HER CYBORG CHAMPION

SUSAN HAYES

DEDICATION

For my Mum and Dad, for all their love and support.

ABOUT THE BOOK

She risked everything to escape from Earth - but her new life came with a cost.

Haven colony is Maggie's new home and her one chance at freedom. Clean water, free air... As far as she's concerned, it's paradise. But getting here meant leaving her best friend behind.

It doesn't take long for her to learn Haven is surrounded by hidden dangers—and the most dangerous of all is a sexy, scarred cyborg named Striker.

Humans took everything from him. His family, his friends, even his voice. Why would he trust one of them with anything?

Striker just wants to live quietly. The wild places beyond the colony are his sanctuary, a place he can go to forget about his past and the ones he failed to protect.

He intended to stay clear of the human colonists. Then, one of them started entering *his* woods. Maggie isn't like the others. She's determined, beautiful, and unaware of the dangers prowling the forest.

He never wanted to be responsible for anyone again, but the flame-haired beauty needs him more than she knows… and he might need her more than he thinks.

PROLOGUE

BEYOND THE EDGE of civilized space is a newly colonized planet. It's a haven for the homeless, the hopeful, and those dreaming of freedom.

The beings who live here might be different species from vastly different worlds - but they all have one thing in common. Whoever they are, and wherever they came from, Haven is now their home.

The land is uncharted. The dangers are unknown. It's a world full of possibilities – for those willing to risk everything.

Welcome to Haven Colony.

1

———

MAGGIE LOOKED DOWN at the empty seat beside her and felt a pang of worry. Jade should be here. This was supposed to be *their* adventure, but her best friend had vanished the night before they were due to report for their flight, leaving her to make the voyage to Haven colony on her own.

The shuttle bounced and rocked a little as they descended into the planet's atmosphere. Some of the others stirred uneasily in their seats, but over the last few weeks Maggie had come to trust Vardarian technology more than anything put together by human hands.

All the tech had operated perfectly, which was a new experience for her. From the air purifiers to the food dispensers, everything had performed its tasks quickly, quietly, and with no malfunctions. As far as she was concerned, any crew who could keep an entire ship running that smoothly could be trusted to bring her safely to her new home. She leaned back in her comfortable chair and enjoyed the ride.

"We'll be through the clouds shortly. If you select the

forward view on your screens, you should get your first look at the planet Liberty any moment now," N'tash, their Vardarian pilot, announced from the flight deck.

The energy in the shuttle's cabin quickly shifted from worry to anticipation. Everyone not already watching their monitors activated them and stared at the thick white clouds still obscuring the view. A buzz of excited chatter filled the air. Maggie shared in the sentiment, but she had no one to talk to, so she stayed quiet and kept her eyes locked on her viewscreen.

She'd expected the clouds to thin out gradually. They didn't. One moment everything was gray and the next she saw a breathtaking expanse of blue. Water. No, she realized as her mind absorbed the scale of what she was looking at. An ocean. A vast, glorious stretch of unpolluted water. The reality of what was happening finally hit her.

She'd made it.

No more recycled air for her. She could bask in real daylight, and the water she drank would be so fresh it might have never been inside another being. If the price for that freedom was a lifetime bond with a pair of alien strangers? She'd gladly pay it.

Again, she looked over at the empty seat beside her and wished Jade was here. This had been her idea. *Where was she?*

Leaving her best friend behind had been the hardest decision of Maggie's life, but in the end, she'd stuck to their plan. It was how they'd made it this far. No matter how *fraxxed* up things got, they got through it by sticking to the plan. So when she'd read Jade's last message, she'd known exactly what she had to do, even if she didn't want to do it.

. . .

Haul ass. You know the drill. See you when I see you. Stay safe. J.

P.S. Peaches.

The last line was a code word. It meant Jade had sent something to Maggie's implant. It was black market tech—undetectable to most scans and completely inaccessible to the one carrying it. Whatever data she was carrying, she couldn't read it.

No other details were in the message, not even a hint as to what had gone wrong. But that was by design. The less the other knew, the less they could give away if they were caught. So instead of going looking for Jade, Maggie had downed her drink, dropped some corporate vouchers on the table, and gone to do the job they were supposed to do together—visit every secret cache they'd set up over the years and take what they needed. New clothes. Hard currency. Food. She'd gathered up enough for both of them. She'd still had hope Jade would find a way to join her at the last minute.

That hope was gone now. They were about to land at the colony, and she hadn't heard from Jade again.

The shuttle had barely touched down before she unbuckled her harness and was on her feet, ready to go. She'd attended every class, worked out daily to build up the muscles she'd need for the higher gravity, and she'd spent as much time as she could in the sims to get over her brain's distrust of open spaces.

It didn't bother her as much as it did some of the other women. She guessed it was because she'd spent a little time near the outer walls. As a kid, she'd snuck out a few times to play in the small gaps between the buildings and the shields protecting them.

She bounced on her toes as two Vardarian females handed out sunglasses and advised them all to move slowly, especially on the stairs.

"If you're feeling anxious, don't look up. You'll have plenty of time to watch the clouds later, once you're settled in," Vixi reminded them all in perfect Galactic Standard.

It was hard to remember why Maggie had been nervous around them the first few days on board. Every Vardarian she'd met was friendly, helpful, and spoke her language. Vixi was the Vardarian version of a doctor and one of the few unmated aliens on board. She took her duties seriously and made sure everyone took their meds and did their exercises every day.

Maggie and the other women had all been taking language lessons because they couldn't be implanted with translation devices right away. Those would come after they received their nanotech injections, six months from now or after being claimed by one of the colony's males, whichever came first.

Right now she didn't care about nanotech, males, or language lessons. She just wanted to get off the shuttle and stand in the unshielded sun for the first time. It might not be the star she'd orbited for the first part of her life, but as far as she was concerned, sunlight was sunlight. Earth was her former home. Her future was here, on Liberty… or it would be as soon as they let her off this *vething* shuttle.

"We're waiting for the unmated males to move farther away. Some of them let their curiosity get the better of their common sense," Tanas announced.

There was a chorus of nervous laughter. They'd have

time to settle in before the unclaimed males would be allowed close enough to scent them. If their mates were out there, they weren't going to meet them for a few weeks yet.

Vixi opened the door. Sunlight streamed in, making her silver skin gleam.

Maggie tried to imagine what that would feel like but couldn't. She'd find out soon, though she belatedly saw her mistake. She should have snagged a seat near the front, but going to the back of the shuttle had seemed like an easy way to avoid conversation. Now, everyone was ahead of her, which meant she'd be the last one off.

Fraxx.

Vixi stepped out first, followed by Tanas. Irisa stayed by the door, providing encouragement and support as the women filed out one-by-one. All the Vardarians had been welcoming and kind, but Maggie liked Irisa the best. The golden-skinned female was always laughing, and despite the fact she was over one hundred years old, she still looked at her mates with unabashed desire and affection. It gave Maggie hope that maybe someone in the universe might look at her that way someday.

She finally reached the doorway and Irisa.

"Take a breath, Maggie. This world can wait a little longer."

"I won't, though. I've waited my whole life for this."

Irisa laughed. "You're not going to do this slowly. Are you?"

"Nope."

The female shook her head in mock dismay and then peeked out the door. "Kara is almost clear. Give her a few more seconds."

"You're not going to tell me to be careful?"

"Why would I do that?" Irisa stepped back. "Go. And welcome home."

Caught up in a moment of joy, Maggie launched herself out the door and into her new life. She'd spent the trip worried that someone would realize the randomized draw hadn't been random at all. No one had noticed. She was here. And no matter what happened now, she'd find a way to stay.

He shouldn't be here.

Striker didn't know what had drawn him to the edge of the landing field to watch the shuttle land. The beings on board were strangers. Worse, they were humans.

The thrusters kicked on as the shuttle neared the ground. The ground beneath his feet trembled, and the branches above him shifted in a sudden breeze thick with the scent of ozone. A shower of leaves fell around him in a flurry of red, gold, and purple, and Striker allowed himself to be distracted by the colorful display.

This was the first time the colony had experienced autumn, and he was enjoying the changes to his woods. Not that they were actually *his*, but given that he was one of the few beings who preferred the silence of nature to the bustle and thrum of Haven's streets, he liked to think of them that way.

Would any of the humans on board want to explore beyond the colony? Veth, he hoped not. He didn't want them intruding there. Besides, the woods were dangerous. Especially for an unenhanced human female. They had no implants. No nanotech. Hell, it was a safe bet none of them had ever been outside before. They were from Earth, transported here as refugees from a dying planet.

Typical. The humans had destroyed their home and then abandoned the least desirable members of their species to die a slow death along with their homeworld. Humans corrupted everything they touched, which was why he didn't think of himself as human. He was a cyborg.

The shuttle settled on its landing pad. A few seconds later, the engines powered down. They'd be disembarking soon and taking their first steps on a new planet, under a strange sky. Haven's newest colonists. That's how the leadership council referred to them. As if they were just like the others who called this place home. They weren't. They were potential mates for the males of Haven—Vardarian and cyborg alike.

Not him, though. He had no interest in pairing up with a woman for more than a night of mutual pleasure. He could find willing company among the cyborg women, as well as a few of the unclaimed Vardarian females. A committed relationship was not on his radar, and if he lost his mind someday and decided he wanted something more, it would not be with a human. They'd already taken too much from him. He didn't trust any of them.

He caught a flash of bright pink hair among the crowd standing near the tarmac and amended his thought. At least one human had proven herself trustworthy—Phaedra Kari. The first of her species to be claimed by a pair of Vardarian males, she was now the consort of the Vardarian prince who had helped found the colony. Phaedra was smart, loyal and fiercely protective of Haven and everyone in it, particularly the cyborgs she'd helped to bring here.

They might have been left in cryo-stasis forever if she hadn't fought for them.

A message came through his internal comms channel. *"You know I can see you. Right?"* It was Edge, the unofficial leader of the colony's cyborg population.

Striker scanned the crowd, using his cybernetic eye to zoom in until he picked out Edge near the back of the group gathered to greet the new arrivals. *"Of course you can see me. It's not like I'm hiding up here."*

"Yet you're lurking in the trees instead of joining us," Edge said.

"Lurking is not the same as hiding. I was in the area and heard the shuttle's engine. Thought I'd check it out."

It was a lie, and they both knew it. He also knew the other cyborg wouldn't call him on it. It wasn't only because Edge had command functionality embedded in his programming that they looked to him for leadership. He was a surly bastard, but he knew what his people needed from him. In Striker's case, that was simple. He wanted to be left the *fraxx* alone.

"You're welcome to stand with us," was all Edge said.

"I know." There wasn't anything else to say. Not that he'd actually said anything out loud. He did most of his communication by his internal channels. His voice—what was left of it—wasn't something he used often.

There was a minor stir of activity on the tarmac as the handful of Vardarian males present launched themselves into the air and flew back to the colony. The council had decreed that the males couldn't approach the women until they'd had a chance to adjust to their new home. Once a Vardarian caught their mate's scent, things happened quickly, with all three falling into a mating fever that couldn't be denied without risking the sanity and even the lives of everyone involved. For now, the winged wonders would have to wait to find out if their mate was among the handful of women aboard.

An opening appeared on the side of the shuttle. Even at this distance, his enhanced senses allowed him to hear the hiss of air as the seal broke and the pressure inside the cabin equalized. A set of stairs unfolded from beneath the doorway, extending down to the tarmac.

Striker caught himself leaning forward and forced himself to take a step back. He wasn't interested. Not really. They were humans. If they were lucky, maybe this first batch wouldn't be able to acclimatize, and they'd end the refugee program before any more arrived. That could happen for plenty of reasons—the higher gravity, cultural differences, the change in climate. Hell, the fact there was a climate at all would unsettle some of them. It had taken some cyborgs months to adjust to weather and an open sky. They'd been created after the war and spent their lives as research subjects on a space station. These humans had lived their lives inside an enclosed system. If they couldn't adapt, they wouldn't send more here. They could find some other planet to live on. Somewhere far away from him.

A Vardarian female appeared first. Her silver skin gleamed in the sun as she unfurled her wings and glided down to the tarmac instead of taking the stairs. Another Vardarian female exited and flew down to join her companion. They both raised their hands and beckoned. For a moment, nothing happened. Then, a human woman stepped out, her eyes shielded by a pair of tinted glasses. She looked around in obvious wonder and then gripped the railing and descended with deliberate care.

Others followed, each of them wearing the same

glasses and moving at the same slow pace as they tested their legs against the new gravity. There was a gap in the flow after the eighth woman left the shuttle. There were supposed to be ten women, though he'd heard a rumor one had dropped out before they'd departed Earth. Had only eight made the trip?

Number nine waited until the woman in front of her was on the tarmac before exploding out the door like a comet. She let out a whoop, threw a leg over one railing, and slid down it to the ground, hitting hard enough to fall to her knees on impact. She bounced back to her feet, threw out her arms, and spun in a circle, her face lifted to the sky. Beaming and laughing, the woman danced, her red hair glowing like fire in the afternoon sun.

Striker couldn't take his eyes off her.

He'd witnessed the arrival of hundreds of Vardarian colonists and had been present when many of his cyborg brethren were roused from cryo-sleep and told that their nightmare was over—that they were free. None of them had reacted with the joy of this small human. Was she intoxicated? Had her mind broken during the journey?

He used his implant to get a closer look at her. If he hadn't, he would have missed the moment she took off her glasses to wipe the tears from her cheeks. She looked up again and called out, "You did it, Jaybird. You got me here. Wherever you are, thank you, now get your ass here as fast as you can."

None of the other women reacted to her outburst. In fact, they seemed to be working hard to ignore her. That caught his interest more than her wild antics. *She's an outsider. Like me.*

He knocked the errant thought away like he was swatting an insect. She wasn't like him. She was human.

Tiny. Unenhanced. She would barely come to his shoulder. She was nothing like him.

He tore his gaze away from the strange little human and stepped back into the forest, fading into the sun-dappled shadows. He had work to do, and he'd wasted enough of his day already. The humans were nothing more than a distraction. He had a home to build, traps to check, and the vast wilds of this world to explore. The humans could have the colony. The woods were his, and no fragile human woman was going to take them from him. They'd ruined their own world. He would not let them destroy this one.

2

MAGGIE DASHED the last few meters to the woods. If she was spotted, she'd get yet another lecture about the dangers of leaving the colony alone and unarmed.

She almost made it.

"Maggie, where are you going?"

Fraxx.

"I need to clear my head." It was true enough. After a lifetime of noise and crowds, she had discovered that a walk in the woods was a balm to her soul. She could think out here. She could breathe.

"It's dangerous out there. You've been to the briefings. Plenty of wildlife out there would be happy to put humanity on the menu." Skye, one of the cyborg women charged with helping the human colonists adapt, joined her in the shadow of the trees.

Humanity. The casual mention of the word made her want to wince. Skye hadn't meant it as an insult, though. If she had issues with humans, she kept it well hidden and had done her best to help Maggie and the others adjust to life at the colony.

Not everyone she'd met was so welcoming. Some of them were downright hostile. She understood their reasons, but it frustrated her that they couldn't understand that anyone still on Earth was as much a victim of the corporations as the cyborgs had been.

"There's an easy solution to that problem. If it's so dangerous out there, give me a blaster so I can protect myself."

Skye laughed. "Have you ever fired one before?"

"Well, no. But I'm a quick study." Energy weapons were heavily restricted back on Earth. While she'd bent and outright broken plenty of rules, she'd never messed with that one. Only security forces and the hardest criminals carried that kind of weaponry. She fell somewhere between the two.

"That's what I thought. No blaster for you."

"I'm going to need to learn how to use one eventually." Maggie hefted the walking stick she carried. She'd sharpened the top into a point, but that wouldn't help her against a ghost cat or a *kopaki*.

"When you've finished your probation period, yes. You've only been here a few weeks. Technically, you're not supposed to be in the woods at all."

Maggie grinned. "The rules state I'm supposed to stay on this side of the river for now. There's nothing in there about staying inside the boundaries of the colony."

Skye was quiet for a moment.

Maggie stayed silent and resettled the pack she carried to a more comfortable spot while she waited for the other woman to finish scanning her copy of the rules. At first, the momentary silences had seemed strange. Now, she knew it meant they were either talking on an internal channel or scanning their vast data files for information.

Eventually Skye sighed. "If I didn't know better, I'd swear you were a lawyer instead of a bartender."

"Hardly. Didn't have the grades. And even as a kid, I knew better than to sign my life over to a corporation."

Skye nodded, her lips pressed in a tight line. "At least you had a choice."

"Not much of one. The alternative was living like a rat in an overcrowded maze, fighting for recycled scraps and trying to scrape together enough hard scrip to get off the planet."

"Any regrets?" Skye had asked.

"Yeah. I regret that no one will give me a blaster so I can protect myself from the more aggressive wildlife out there."

"I meant about coming here. Some of the others..." Skye looked back toward the collection of buildings where the human women were currently living.

"Yeah. Some of them are struggling to deal with the changes." Maggie dropped her voice, knowing the cyborg would hear her clearly. "But that's because they're the ones from the U.C. levels."

"U.C.?"

Context is an interesting thing. You didn't notice it until it wasn't there. Apart from the nine women from Earth, no one on this planet had ever seen a hive city, and none of them had any idea how they worked.

"Upper center." Maggie held out her hands, palms down, one over the other. "More than half of Athens Two is underground. If you can afford to live above the dirt, you've got money, influence, or a little of both."

She shifted her hands so they were side by side. "Same for where you live in relation to the walls. The deeper into the center you are, the more protection you have if something fails. Water, air, power all come through the center and out to the walls."

"Ah, so you're saying the women having the hardest time adjusting are the ones who lived the best back on Earth?"

"Exactly."

"And you? Where did you live?"

"As a kid, that depended on who my mom was sleeping with at the time. We made it above ground once or twice, but we were still near the outer walls. As an adult, I lived on the lower levels. Rent was cheaper there."

Skye nodded thoughtfully. "So you adapted and made the best of things. They haven't needed to do that. At least, not to the same extent. Thank you. That's very helpful. I think we're going to need to screen the next group for certain attributes, including adaptability. This place takes some getting used to."

"So does being free."

"Truth." Skye's brow creased. "And freedom means being allowed to make your own choices. Like whether to go into the woods armed with nothing more than a pointy stick and a smart mouth."

"You could give me your—"

"Nope. No blaster. You want to exercise your freedom, you do it without a weapon you don't know how to use. But I'll arrange for weapons training for anyone interested. Starting tomorrow."

"Thank you." Maggie startled them both by moving in and giving the much taller cyborg a one-armed hug. "That means a lot to me."

Skye blinked and then smiled and hugged her back. "You be careful out there. The wildlife aren't the only dangerous things in these woods."

"Vardarians?" She wasn't ready to run into her mates yet, if she had mates on this planet.

"Not all of my brethren are embracing colony life. Some of them prefer the woods. Away from everyone. It's probably safer for both parties that way, but they won't be happy to see you."

"I'll be careful."

"I know you will. See you for the evening meal?"

While all the new colonists had been assigned their own habi-pod with a kitchen and food dispenser, the group would eat dinner together, along with any cyborgs and Vardarian females or mated males who wished to join them. Some meals were quiet, but others were rowdy, enjoyable affairs that felt more like a party.

"What's on the menu?"

"Something called lasagna." Skye shrugged. "Whatever that is."

"Pasta. Meat. Tomato sauce. Lots of cheese. I had it once. The real thing. Cost me a month's wages and it was worth every bite. I will definitely be there for dinner."

"Good. I thought maybe you planned on staying out for a while given the size of the pack you're carrying."

Maggie repeated the line she'd rehearsed until the delivery was perfect. "Nope. This is just the basics in case I get stuck somewhere. Poncho, heat source, food tabs, and water."

"Smart."

"I did my research."

"I can see that. See you at dinner."

Skye left, and Maggie walked into the trees before she exhaled and leaned against the nearest trunk. Lying to a cyborg wasn't easy. They could sense pulse rates and read body language in ways no human could match. So, she hadn't lied. She'd simply practiced a version of the truth, instead—one that didn't mention the other items she carried. She had fuel pellets for a cookstove she'd traded for last week and a thermal blanket someone had thrown out because one corner was torn off.

There was so much waste here it made her head swim. Scraps of food were tossed into composters every day. Anything that wasn't perfect was thrown out and replaced. Things were recycled, yes, but they had an entire planet full of raw materials, and more of everything was brought in by traders all the time. Waste and wealth all around her, so she did what she could to claim some of it for herself. Not stealing. Just taking what had been cast off and doing what she did best—trading up.

Barter and trade were necessary skill sets for people like her, and she was honestly surprised most of the others weren't doing the same thing. She'd seen Nasha combing through the recycling almost every day, and Dani had been out a few times. They traded what they found between the three of them. Nasha was looking for extra food she could stash and materials to make her own clothing. Dani was looking for anything she could trade for *koldar*, the Vardarian currency they used on this world. The others barely went outside. They attended the countless classes on everything from language to Vardarian mating customs and then spent the rest of their time in their habi-pods, sharing news from a place they still called home.

Maggie didn't understand it. They'd all known what they were signing up for. This was their one chance at a fresh start. Why weren't they embracing it?

There had been tens of thousands of entrants. They'd had to do the draw three times to cull out the ones who were too old, too young, or failed their physical exams. The first round had been open to anyone, a sort of experiment to see if the idea could work.

For her and Jade, it had been the chance of a lifetime. If the project continued, there'd be screenings and deliberations to ensure they brought over the ones with the best shot of making the transition. Not even Jade's hacking skills could erase two lifetimes of dubious decisions and occasional brushes with the law. If they hadn't been on the first ship, they'd have never gotten here at all.

She and Jade had spent months planning their escape. They'd gathered information, figured out a plan, and then had to scrap it and start over again more than once. Once they'd come up with their final concept, it took Jade weeks to access the right systems and set everything up. Hacking the list directly was too obvious. Instead, Jade planted a simple subroutine that added variations of their names over time. By the time the draws started, the odds were as good as they could make them without tipping anyone off.

It had worked better than they'd hoped. They'd both won a spot, Maggie in one draw, Jade in another. It was supposed to be their shot. But at the last minute Jade had gone looking for what she called insurance… and then she'd disappeared.

Maggie rubbed at her arm, the one with the implant. She had no way to know for certain, but she suspected that whatever Jade had gone after, she'd found it. That's what her friend had sent to her, and it's what had gotten Jade into trouble.

Worry churned in her stomach and Maggie set out at a brisk walk. She thought better when she was moving. It had always been like that for her, and since she'd started taking the pharma to increase her bone density and accelerate muscle growth, she could go for hours, even in the heavier gravity of Liberty. The food helped, too. She'd never eaten so much, or so well.

Part of her didn't trust that something this good could go on indefinitely. The food would run out. There'd be an attack, an illness, or some sort of natural disaster. When that happened, she needed to be ready. So, she did the same thing she'd done back on Earth. She gathered up what she could find and hid it all where no one else would find it—the woods.

Despite Skye's warning, Maggie hadn't seen anyone else on her walks. All she'd run across were rockclaws and squeakers. The squeakers were this biosphere's version of rodents. Granted, they had green fur, red eyes, and hissed a lot, but otherwise they were pretty much the same creatures she knew from Earth.

The rockclaws were something else entirely. Massive crab-like creatures, they lumbered through the forest like six-legged tanks. Their claws were the size of her head, strong enough to break bones if they got a hold of you. They weren't aggressive, though. If she left them alone, they were happy to do the same. It helped that they were so brightly colored they were easy to spot. She'd seen yellow, blue, and the occasional pink ones trundling through the trees. If one got too close, she prodded it with her walking stick until it changed direction.

The stick was handy for pushing bloodvine out of her way, too. The stuff sensed body heat and contracted around anything it found, tearing at it with hundreds of sharp thorns, but it didn't react to the wood. Still, she'd like to have an energy weapon, too. In case something bigger came along.

Until that happened, she'd stick a little closer to the colony. The more dangerous wildlife stayed away from Haven, knowing the biggest predators on the planet lived there.

She hefted her pack and picked her way through the woods, carefully counting her steps as she went. The spot she wanted wasn't far now. Ten more minutes and she'd have her next cache safely stashed. Then she could head back for dinner. Easy-peasy.

∾

She was back again.

Striker wasn't sure what to make of the little redhaired human who kept coming back to his woods. She'd been hiding things out here. He'd found two of her stashes and gone through the contents. Food, water, and equipment—most of it out of date or imperfect. It didn't make sense. Food was plentiful. Equipment could be made to order. Yet she came out here every few days and added to her stockpile of junk.

The first time he'd seen her out here, he'd followed her to make sure she wasn't doing anything that might jeopardize the colony. Now, she was a puzzle he wanted to solve. He'd set up a sensor to tell him when anyone entered this area. So far, she was the only one who wandered more than a few meters from home. He wasn't sure if that said more about her or the other human women.

The humans stayed together for the most part, but not the one he'd learned was called Maggie. His impression that she was an outsider had only strengthened since the first time he'd seen her dancing in the sunlight outside the shuttle. She spent more time with the cyborg women than her own kind. That was a mark in her favor. She also had no idea how much danger she was in every time she set foot in his woods.

Maggie had wandered into a ghost cat's hunting grounds one time. He'd run it off before it attacked her. The woman had figured out how to deal with the rockclaws and bloodvine, but a stick wasn't going to protect her from any of the larger predators. She should be armed if she was coming out here, yet no one seemed inclined to stop her visits.

Did they want her to get killed? It was one way to deter more colonists, sure. But it might also cause problems the colony didn't need. So, he shadowed her, kept her safe, and tried to figure out what the *fraxx* she was up to.

All he knew about her was her name. Maggie Piper. He hadn't asked anyone about her. That would require talking, and he didn't do much of that anymore. He touched the scar at his throat. The only ones he wanted to talk to were long gone.

Once she was close enough, he broke into a run so he got to her destination before she did. He did a quick scan for threats and then leaped up into a tree on the far side of the clearing to settle in and wait.

This was where she'd been coming the last few trips. To a rotting tree in the center of a small clearing. Bloodvine lay all over the forest floor here, but she'd learned to wear heavy boots and use her staff to sweep most of it out of her way. She always got a few cuts, though, and the blood was absorbed into the soil to be turned into nutrients for the vines. She hadn't noticed yet, but more of the vines lined the path she took to the tree. More vines meant more cuts, and more blood meant more vines. A few more trips and anyone coming through here would be able to see what he could—clear signs that someone was visiting this place.

As smart as she was, she didn't know the rules of her new home, and she couldn't see all the threats. She had no idea what to look for. He did.

While he waited, he scanned the woods for heat signatures. No predators. Just a juvenile rockclaw wandering through the underbrush. Even Maggie's limited senses would be able to hear it and stay clear.

Maggie arrived a few minutes later, counting out her steps as she came. It was a rudimentary way to navigate, but it worked well enough. She was smart and capable for a human, and as much as he hated to admit it, she was attractive. She'd filled out since her arrival, her curves more pronounced now, and she had a vitality to her that appealed to him—at least, from a distance, and that's all he was interested in.

If Edge or any of the others knew he was following a human woman around, they'd never let him hear the end of it. And it wasn't like they were ever going to meet. He was just doing his part to protect the future of the colony.

Maggie paused to check her surroundings and then moved into the open space. She went slowly, sweeping her crudely made staff from side to side to clear a path through the vines.

He didn't see the danger until she was almost to the rotting tree. Then he noticed a glimmer of heat he'd somehow missed the first time.

Bark spider.

Instinct was faster than conscious thought. He'd thrown the knife before he had gotten around to deciding if he was going to help her. It struck the creature dead center, pinning its flattened body to the trunk of the tree.

It shrieked and flailed its legs in an obscene dance as it died, and Maggie stumbled backward with a choking cry.

"What the hell? Who? Where!" the questions fell from her lips in an adrenaline-fueled torrent.

He didn't answer any of them. He jumped down from the tree and walked right past her to retrieve his knife from the corpse. The moment he pulled the blade out, the body dropped to the ground. It was the size of a dinner tray, perfectly mottled to blend in against the bark of a tree. It was an ambush predator with a nasty bite he'd experienced firsthand when he was still learning about the dangers of this place.

If it had bitten her, Maggie would have suffered an agonizing but quick death. That was why he'd revealed himself. No one deserved to die like that, in pain and alone.

"You!" A small fist smacked his bicep.

He turned and looked down at the human female with surprise.

"You could have killed me throwing that thing!"

He shook his head, bending down to wipe the blade clean before sheathing the knife. He straightened, pointing to the dead bark spider and then at her.

She scowled. "That thing would have hurt me?"

He raised two fingers into a semblance of fangs and then struck at his own arm. After that, he pointed to her again, and then made a falling over gesture with his hand.

"Killed me? It's venomous? Well, *fraxx*. No one mentioned anything like that in our classes."

He snorted. They didn't teach it because not many knew they existed. Everyone was so busy trying to get the defense platform up and the colony established before winter came. There hadn't been much time or inclination to explore the world they'd claimed.

"You don't talk?" she asked.

He shook his head and tapped the scar at his throat.

Her brow crumpled into a frown. "But you're a cyborg. Right? Can't you heal almost anything?"

He gave a slight shake of his head.

"It must have been a nasty injury. I'm sorry."

That surprised him. The humans he'd met didn't apologize for anything. Ever. He almost spoke then to tell her it wasn't a big deal.

He settled for a shrug and then pointed to her pack, then the tree where she'd hidden her other things.

"You've been watching me." It wasn't a question.

He nodded once.

"Why?"

Frustration rolled through him. "Because I think you're up to something and I want to know what the *fraxx* it is," wasn't something he could communicate effectively with signs.

"Right. You can't talk." She moved away from the corpse of the spider and shrugged out of her pack. "So, let me work through this and you let me know if I get anything wrong."

Another nod.

"You've been watching me."

Nod again.

"How long? Days? Weeks?"

He nodded at weeks.

"Okay. Going to be honest, that's a little disconcerting."

Striker snickered.

"Oh sure, you can laugh. You're not the one being stalked."

He pointed to the dead spider and then gestured around them, moving his hands to mimic pinchers and claws.

She paled. "You've been protecting me? From things like that? Dammit! This is why I asked Skye for a blaster. I need to be able to defend myself."

If she'd asked for a blaster, why wasn't she carrying one? He pointed to his and then to the empty spot on her belt where most beings would carry a weapon.

"We're not allowed. Not yet. That kind of weaponry is restricted on Earth and none of us know how to use one."

If the wind had gusted at that moment, it might have knocked him over. She didn't know how to use an energy weapon? She was human. The most violent species in the known galaxy.

"You look surprised." She tipped her head and her red hair tumbled over her shoulders like living flame. "You don't know much about humans. At least, not ones from Earth." A handful of humans were on Liberty already—two females and one half-Torski male. None of them were from Earth.

He pointed to her and then flicked up a finger.

That made her grin. "I'm your first. Huh?"

He chuckled. It came out sounding more like a rusty engine than an expression of humor, but she laughed along with him. It felt surprisingly good, and for a second he forgot that she was human and not to be trusted.

The moment didn't last. When the laughter died away, he pointed to her bag and then to the tree, and then he raised both hands in question. What was she doing out here, and why was she doing it?

3

———

Maggie wasn't sure if this was a nightmare or the best dream ever. If she went by the giant dead bug that had tried to eat her, she was in nightmare territory. On the other hand, she'd been saved from the bug by a tall, blond, panty-meltingly hot man with a sexy as sin smile and no inclination to talk. Definitely a dream come true.

He was also more than capable of getting his message across with his nimble fingers and charming smile. It was probably a good thing the man couldn't speak. She already wanted to climb him like a ladder. If he talked to her, there was a dangerously high chance she'd spontaneously combust instead of answering his question.

"I didn't steal any of it. It's mine."

He arched a brow but otherwise didn't move.

"It's all stuff I recovered from recycling. Or I traded what I found for what I needed. You all throw out a lot of perfectly useable items. It's wasteful." She couldn't keep the acid out of that last word.

His expression softened. It was subtle, but she saw it.

She'd been reading people since she was a child, learning who was a threat and who was a potential ally. She didn't know which camp this man would fall into, but he was giving her a chance to explain herself. That counted for something.

When he made a "go on" gesture with his hands and then pointed to the tree, she continued.

"You want to know why I'm bringing it out here?"

The big blond nodded.

"Because where I'm from, it's not smart to leave everything you own in one place. If someone else finds it, they're happy and you're *fraxxed*."

He nodded, gestured to the tree, and held up one finger. Then he pointed in the direction of her other hiding spots and raised several more fingers, giving her an inquiring look.

Crap. He knew what she was doing and where her caches were.

"You're asking me why so many?" She put his question into words to be sure she knew what he wanted to know.

He nodded.

"Okay. You're not going to understand, but here's the truth. This place is too good to be true. One day I'm going to wake up and it's all going to be gone. I don't know how, or what *fraxxed* up thing will happen, but it will happen. That's the way the universe works. When that day comes, I'll be ready." She squared her shoulders and met his gaze. "Unless you're going to report me? Or take this stuff for yourself. Then, I guess I'm screwed, and not in the fun way." She hadn't meant to say that last bit. Telling the truth must have messed up her verbal filters.

When he reached for her pack, she froze. He was going

to take it from her and she could do nothing to stop him. This was a cyborg—a man designed from the DNA up to be a fighting machine. She might as well pick a fight with a mountain.

To her surprise, he didn't pull it out of her grasp. He set his hand on it and then withdrew and pointed to the tree.

"You're letting me keep it?"

A single nod.

"Why?" The moment she asked the question, she knew he wouldn't be able to explain. "Sorry. You can't really answer that. Can you? Maybe if we had a tablet, you could type out an answer."

He shook his head and raised his empty hands.

"No tablet. Well, that will make this trickier." She set down the pack and held out her hand to him. "I'm Maggie. Maggie Piper. Can you at least tell me your name?"

For a moment, the big cyborg didn't move. He eyed her hand like it was another of those venomous bugs. Then, he took her hand in his much larger one and shook it.

When he let go, the warmth of his touch lingered on her skin. "Name?"

He whipped out the knife and stepped over to the rotting tree. With quick strokes, he carved something into the wood. It was easy to read even from where she stood, the letters in Galactic Standard.

"Striker. That's your name?" She smiled. "I like it."

His answering smile was hot enough to melt hull plating and fry the last of her filters. "Is there a reason why every cyborg I've met looks like a cross between a war god and a holo-vid actor? Did you all win the genetic lottery?"

The moment the words left her lips, she realized her error. What was a joke to her was a reality for Striker and the other cyborgs. They were the result of genetic manipulation, along with behavior programming, controls, and enough cybernetic tech to power a starship.

Striker's lip curled up in a silent snarl.

She was so *fraxxed*. Instinctively she dropped her head and rounded her shoulders, falling into a submissive pose that she resented with every cell in her body. But it was the only thing she could think to do, a throwback to her life on Earth. A life she thought she'd left behind. "I'm sorry. I spoke without thinking. I didn't mean…"

He moved in close enough she saw his boots in her limited field of vision. She braced, waiting for the inevitable blow.

It didn't come.

Maggie held her breath and kept her head down. She'd been lulled into a false sense of security before. She knew better than to think this was over. Insults required a response, and Striker had been insulted. She'd seen it in his eyes.

When his hand touched her shoulder, she managed not to flinch away, but he didn't grab her. Slowly, he moved his hand up, his fingers brushing over her hair and then settling under her chin. He applied only enough pressure to make her lift her head, and she looked up to stare into his deep blue eyes. She saw no anger there.

She let out a slow breath. "You're not going to hurt me?"

His lip curled and his eyes narrowed. Dammit, she'd managed to insult him again.

"I… I don't understand."

Striker huffed in frustration and moved back.

"You're angry. Because I thought you were going to hit me?"

A sharp nod.

"That's what happens when someone like me angers someone bigger or tougher. At least, that's how it works where I'm from."

Striker pointed to the sky and then slashed a hand through the air before pointing to the ground.

That was easy enough to understand. "You're saying that I'm not on Earth anymore. But how am I supposed to know what things are really like here? It all seems too good to be true."

Silence fell.

She waited.

Eventually Striker made a sound somewhere between a sigh and snort. It was a perfect expression of emotion without saying a single word.

The tension between them faded, and she relaxed. It was going to be okay. "Yeah. You're not the first one to accuse me of making them feel that way."

He grinned, pointed to her pack, and then made a gesture like he was opening it.

"You want to know what I brought? It's not much. Fuel pellets for a camp stove and a thermal blanket someone tossed out." She fished the items out and showed them to him. He looked over each one and then handed them back.

All but the last item.

It was a brick of food tabs she'd traded for. The things were barely edible and tasted like stale cardboard dipped in dust, but they were packed with nutrients. A single cube of the stuff was equal to a full meal, and the tabs would keep for years if their wrappings weren't breached.

Striker jabbed a finger at something written on the side.

"I can't see that from here. The print is too small."

He held it out to her, scowling.

It only took a second to see what his issue was. "Yeah. They're past their expiry date. It's fine. All that means is they'll slowly lose some of their potency over time. They're still edible."

The look he shot her could have gone in the dictionary as the definition of dubious.

"I've been eating stale food tabs for years and never had a problem. These are emergency supplies. If I'm reduced to eating this crap, we've got bigger problems than the date on the package."

Striker grudgingly handed over the last package.

"So glad I have your approval," she muttered and turned toward the spot where she'd hidden the rest of her stash. A thought hit her and she froze, frantically scanning the tree for anymore of the camouflaged bugs.

"Please tell me there's nothing else on or in this tree that's going to try and kill me."

The next thing she knew, Striker had taken her pack and shouldered his way past her. He placed the items inside the tree for her and then handed back the empty bag.

"You're not worried about getting bitten?"

He curled two fingers into fangs, tapped his forearm with them, and then shrugged.

"Ah. I forgot about your medi-bots. The nanotech protects you from the poison. Nice. I can't get that for months. Guess I better hope I don't run into anymore of those things until then."

Striker walked two fingers across his forearm and then pointed in the direction of the colony. Then, he held up a hand in a clear sign to stop.

"You're suggesting I go back to Haven and stay there? No. Not happening. I like being out here." She waved around them at the forest. "It's beautiful. And quiet. I've been locked up inside a hive city my entire life. Until I came here, I'd never seen a tree, never mind a forest full of them. I'd rather die out here than live safely inside the colony. That's not why I came all this way."

He watched her intently, his blue eyes looking almost turquoise in the fading light, but didn't sign anything. He just looked at her.

Feeling slightly uncomfortable, Maggie slipped the pack over her shoulder and then looked up at the darkening sky. "I should be getting back. Skye's expecting me to show up for the communal dinner. You're welcome to join us."

He shook his head sharply, one large hand slashing through the air.

"No dinner. Gotcha. Is it the company or the food you're avoiding?"

He flicked up a finger.

"First one. The company. Not a fan of crowds. Huh?" she asked.

Again, Striker shook his head.

Okay. So, big, blond and nonverbal wasn't a social creature. Not a surprise. He had to be one of the cyborgs Skye had warned her about. Though, he didn't seem to have a problem with her. Hell, if he hadn't killed that thing, it would have bitten her. Still, it didn't hurt to ask. "You don't mind my being out here. Do you? I mean, this is sort of your space. Right?"

His eyes widened and something flickered deep in their depths. Then he smiled and her heart did a triple flip in her chest. Holy *fraxx*, he was hot.

After a moment, he nodded, one hand sweeping out to encompass the woods.

She took it as permission. "Thank you. For everything. I just realized I never thanked you for saving my life. I owe you for that. If you need anything. Ever. I will help any way I can."

That earned her another dubious look.

It rankled.

"What? You don't think there's anything I could do for you?" She glared at him. "I've got skills."

Striker tapped the butt of his blaster, then the hilt of his knife, and then pointed to the dead bug. Its legs were starting to curl and stir in the evening breeze, giving the impression it was still alive.

The big guy had a point. "Okay. So my skill set doesn't apply to my current situation. I'm working on that. I have to learn things the hard way. Not like you. One upload and you know everything there is to know about anything you want. It doesn't work that way for us. It's going to take me time to figure things out. But I will. That's one of my skills. I can adapt."

She turned on her heel and walked back the way she'd come. Striker fell in beside her. He wasn't on her pathway and the vines tried to ensnare him, but whatever his pants were made of, the thorns couldn't penetrate the fabric and he strolled through it like the vines weren't there. She couldn't even ask him what the material was. There was no way he'd be able to tell her.

"You're coming with me?" she asked.

He nodded.

"Making sure I get back in one piece?"

He didn't bother to acknowledge that question. They both knew the answer, and she was grateful for the company. Today, the woods didn't seem as welcoming as they had been before she'd known about the damn bugs.

By the time they were within sight of the colony, he'd pointed out several more of the multi-legged nightmares. She knew what to look for now. They were mottled to blend in with the tree bark, but it wasn't a perfect match.

A few meters away from the tree line, Striker stopped.

"Thank you. Tonight I'll sharpen my stick some more. Next time I see one of those things, it's getting skewered."

In answer, Striker indicated his knife and mimicked throwing it.

"That's another skill I'll have to learn, eventually. Slowly. With a lot of practice. Until then, it's probably best I don't start hurling pointy objects around."

Striker chuckled, nodded, and then held out his hand.

She hesitated, not sure what he wanted. His stance was relaxed, his fingers slightly curled. When she didn't move, he moved his hand forward a little.

A handshake. That's all it was. She felt a little foolish as she gripped his hand for a moment. His roughened fingers engulfed her hand and a tiny thrill chased down her spine. Did he want to hold her hand? She'd be quite happy to let him.

Hell, the way he looked, she'd be happy to give him just about any part of her he wanted.

It had been a long time since she'd felt safe enough with a guy to consider letting him get close, but something about Striker made her believe she could trust him. Or maybe she wanted to trust someone. Jade had left a huge hole in her life when she vanished, and so far Maggie hadn't found any trace or hint of where she might have gone. If she was going to find her friend, she was going to need help, and she missed having someone to watch her back.

Not that she expected Striker to be much assistance in tracking down an errant human. He couldn't speak and clearly preferred the company of the forest to beings of any species. But he *had* watched over her. Protected her without her ever knowing he was there. It was a rare man who took action without wanting credit for it. And he was alone, like she was—an outsider.

When he withdrew his hand, she almost moved with him, chasing the warmth of his touch. Almost.

"You're sure you won't come to dinner?" she asked.

He shook his head and pointed back toward the woods.

"I get it. I'm in it for the food, not the company. They're a noisy bunch."

To her surprise, he winked at her, gestured to himself, and then touched a finger to his lips.

"You are not noisy at all. Which makes you good company." She decided to take a chance. "Will I see you again?"

He nodded, and a sense of deep satisfaction rolled through her. He was going to trust her. It was a start. To what, she had no idea.

The door to the hall opened and the chatter of female voices poured out. "I'll be along in a minute. I want to see if Maggie made it back yet."

Skye was looking for her. Maggie turned toward the noise but then looked back to Striker.

More accurately, she looked at the spot where he'd been standing. He'd vanished. Without so much as a whisper of noise. "No wonder I didn't know he was following me."

"Thanks again," she said in a slightly louder voice. She didn't know if he could hear her or not, but she didn't want Skye to overhear her. If Striker had wanted the other cyborg to know he was there, he'd have stayed. That was fine with her. He could be her little secret, at least for now.

The next time she went into the woods, she'd look for him. And she'd bring him something to thank him for his help. If he didn't like company, he must live out in the wilds, away from everyone.

She'd keep an eye out for something he might be able to use. It was the least she could do for the man who had saved her life.

Striker heard the door open and melted back into the woods. If Skye saw him with Maggie, she'd jump on their internal comm channel and start pestering him with questions. It was clear Maggie hadn't told anyone else what she was doing, and he wasn't going to out her to Skye and the others. They'd see it as a problem to be solved. It wasn't. Maggie was a survivor, and for some beings, that meant planning for every contingency.

He understood that kind of thinking. He was a survivor too. He'd hidden tools and food around his cell and spent days figuring out new ways to create weapons he could use to protect himself and those he needed to protect. It hadn't been enough. They found what he'd hidden and punished him for it. The ones he'd tried to protect had died. Often by his own hand. He'd never forgive himself for those deaths, even though it was the only thing he could do for his batch-siblings.

The bastards at Reamus Research Station had twisted

and broken them, stripped away their humanity with drugs and surgery in their quest for the perfect soldier. Mindless. Soulless. Deadly.

He and his batch-siblings had been created during the war, but unlike most of the other cyborgs, they were never freed. They were sent to Reamus Station instead, trading one hellish existence for another even worse.

Until he'd met Phaedra, he'd thought all humans were the same. Denz and Sevda were part Torski, so Striker assumed their Torski traits made them better. He'd avoided meeting the only other human in the colony. Anya ran the Bar None, a tavern set up at the midpoint of the broad bridge that connected the two sides of the colony. She'd chosen her location well, and the place had become popular with both cyborgs and Vardarians.

Edge kept trying to get him to come try the food there and spend some time with the others. Striker had no interest in doing that. The food dispenser in his home provided him with better food than he'd eaten in his life, and he preferred his own company these days.

Being around the others reminded him of the past, and he kept seeing the faces of all those who hadn't lived long enough to breathe free air. The ones he'd failed.

He broke into a dead run, moving through the trees so quickly his surroundings were nothing but a blur. It wasn't that he was trying to outrun his ghosts. He knew better. They were with him every second of every day and would be until he died. He ran because he could. No walls. No cells. No threats or pain. He could run in any direction he chose for as long as he wanted. Running was how he proved to himself he was still free.

Most times he ran until his mind emptied. Today, that didn't happen. His thoughts kept coming back to Maggie.

The sound of her laughter. The way her hair glowed like flames when the sun caught it. How soft her fingers had felt pressed to his skin.

He'd measured her hand during that moment. She'd never be able to use any of the weapons he carried. They were too big. Too heavy. She'd need something lighter with a grip made for her smaller hands. He slowed and then stopped.

Had he actually considered arming a human? On purpose?

Granted, even armed Maggie was about as much a threat to him as a Terran kitten, but still…

Conversations with himself were one of the side effects of spending so much time alone.

"Arming any human is not a good idea."

Another part of him answered. "She should be allowed to defend herself with more than a *fraxxing* stick."

"If she didn't go out into the woods, she wouldn't need defending."

"She came here to be free. Hiding inside the colony isn't freedom. That's just another kind of prison."

The worst part of these conversations was that no matter how many arguments he won, he lost the same number.

It took less than a second to check his onboard systems and plot the fastest route back to the colony. He'd learned the hard way that the river that divided Haven was too wide for him to jump across no matter how fast he ran, and he didn't feel like swimming today. He'd take one of the outer bridges and hope he didn't run into anyone who'd want to talk.

A hot meal and a hotter shower were in order. After two days in the woods, he was looking forward to both.

Tomorrow he needed to find more material for the project he was working on. Maybe he'd check in with Damos and Tra'var to see if they had any weapons that might fit a human's hand. If they didn't have anything yet, they'd need to start making some soon. The newest colonists were going to need them.

4

___

IT WAS three days before he spotted her in his woods again.

She was moving more cautiously now, using her walking stick to push aside several rockclaws that blocked her path. She sang to herself as she walked, not one song, but snippets of lyrics from a variety of musical genres all mashed together. It should have been annoying.

He thought it was oddly appealing.

This time, Maggie didn't take her usual route straight to the tree. She circled the outside of the clearing, doing a full sweep before choosing an approach that was almost free of bloodvine. She spotted the bark spider while she was still several meters away—an impressive feat for someone who couldn't shift their visual spectrum the way he could.

He thought about stepping in to help her deal with it but decided against it. The spiders were ambush predators. This one wouldn't attack unless she got too close. It was smaller than the last one and had positioned itself closer to the ground. The worst it could do was drop onto her boot, and no way could it penetrate her shoes with its fangs. She was safe enough.

If she was going to survive out here, she'd need to learn how to deal with any threat that came her way. More than that, she'd need to believe she was capable. Confidence was key. He stayed where he was and watched.

She hefted the staff she carried, shifting her grip several times before she was satisfied. Then she braced her feet and drove the point into the bark spider. Her stance was off and her technique was almost nonexistent, but it worked. The creature never knew what hit it.

"See that, Striker? I got it!"

Son of a starbeast. She knew he was there.

He stepped into view.

"Ha! I was right. You were following me. You are really *fraxxing* quiet, though. I didn't hear you at all. How do you do that?"

In answer, he raised his hands and pointed to the barcode on his wrist.

"Right. Cyborg. I forgot."

She forgot? That detail never slipped the mind of someone in the presence of one of his kind. The Vardarians viewed them as fellow warriors worthy of respect simply because of what they were. The humans on Reamus Station had treated them with a mixture of fear and cruelty. He'd never met anyone who had forgotten what he was. Not if they wanted to continue breathing.

He shot her an incredulous look and then gestured to himself. How could she forget what he was?

"You're not happy I forgot you were a cyborg?" She frowned at him like he was the one not making sense. "You're you. Striker. Big. Buff. Blond. Handy with a knife and easy to talk to. If I were to make a list of your attributes, cyborg wouldn't make the top ten."

It was like a ray of sunlight hit him in the middle of his chest—a brief flash of light and warmth that faded before he could identify it. It wasn't a malfunction. But it had been something.

Time to change topics. He pointed to her pack and lifted a hand in query.

"This? More food tabs." She grinned. "And these haven't expired yet. Skye asked me to help her do inventory the last few days. These are my payment for services rendered."

Maggie reached into the bag and pulled out a food pack. "And I made these for you."

When he didn't reach for the carton, she thrust it at him. "It's not going to open itself. Go on. Take it. I wasn't sure you'd be out here, so I was going to leave it with a note for you to find. This is better, though."

He took the sealed container from her. Written on the lid was a short message.

Thank you for saving my ass. I hope you like chocolate.
 M.

"So, do you? Like chocolate, I mean."

He nodded several times but didn't bother looking up. He'd never been given a gift before, and he wanted to know what she'd brought him. What she'd made him.

The aroma hit him the moment he opened the lid. Rich notes of vanilla and cocoa laced with sugar. A lot of sugar. He balanced the box on one hand and pulled the lid aside with the other. Once he saw what was inside, he handed the lid to Maggie and scooped up one of his presents.

Cookies. Chocolate ones full of what looked like chunks of chocolate and nuts. He lifted one in a toast and then took a bite. It tasted better than it smelled.

"Thank you." His words were barely intelligible, but that was as much the fault of the mouthful of food he was talking around as his damaged vocal cords.

"Holy *fraxx*. You can talk?" Maggie's expression shifted from shock to anger in a heartbeat. "You sewage sucking bilge fish! You let me think you couldn't... but you can. Why?"

"Hurts." True enough. Speaking more than a few words irritated the scar tissue. A few sentences and he'd feel like he'd gargled gravel. The doctors said if he used his voice more it would get stronger and the discomfort would fade. He didn't want that. The pain reminded him of the one who'd crushed his throat. The man he'd put down a few seconds later. Dag. His last surviving brother... or what was left of him after the scientists had finished working on him.

"Well, *fraxx*. I'm sorry. I thought..." She shook her head and didn't finish. "Doesn't matter what I thought. So you can speak, but it's easier not to?"

He nodded and then made a decision. "Few words okay."

"Which means you could have told me your name the other day." It wasn't a question.

"Mm-hmm," was his noncommittal reply.

"But you didn't want to."

"Don't talk to strangers."

She laughed. "Even ones whose life you just saved? But you're talking to me now."

"Cookies."

"You like them? I didn't know what to get you as a thank you, and cookies are one of the few things I know how to make."

He had another mouthful of cookie by that point and didn't try to speak again. He just raised his hand and lifted his brows. He wanted her to keep talking.

"Yes, I made them. I convinced the cook to let me use the kitchen for an hour today. In exchange, I taught her the recipe. She was working out how to quadruple the batch sizes when I left. I suspect the colony is about to be flooded with double chocolate chip cookies."

He didn't doubt it. The cyborgs had all been prisoners for years, fed nothing but food tabs and algae broth. Any new food was embraced and devoured, especially sweets. He made a show of tucking the box under his arm.

"Don't worry, no one is going to be coming after your cookies. No one knows I'm giving them to you." She winked at him. "You're my secret. I didn't mention that I saw you out here."

He cocked his head in query.

"Why? Because I didn't want to have to answer a bunch of questions about what I was doing out here. They don't know about..." Maggie gestured to the tree stump. "Not unless you told anyone?"

He shook his head. He hadn't mentioned meeting Maggie. Hell, he hadn't spoken to anyone but her, Edge, and his Vardarian forge master friends all week.

Maggie looked relieved. "How many cookies is it going to cost me to buy your silence?" She grinned at him. "I mean, now that I know you can talk."

"One cookie a day." Not that he planned on telling anyone about Maggie. He was her secret, and she was his.

"So, I've already bought almost two weeks?" Her smile turned wicked. "I was ready to go as high as a dozen a week."

"Sold," he said.

"Oh no. That's not how bartering works. You stated your price, I accepted. The deal is done. A cookie a day."

He pointed to the box, to her, and then to the stump.

She brightened. "You want me to bring them to you here? Sure. I can do that."

He held out his hand to her. She reached out but stopped before making contact.

"If you teach me how to protect myself from things like those bugs, I'll make it a dozen a week."

"Bark spiders." The words tore at his throat. He'd spoken too much today.

"Is that what they're called? Don't they have too many legs to be a spider?"

He shrugged. They were spider-like and spent their time hiding on tree bark. The name fit well enough.

"And you didn't respond to my offer. Lessons for baked goods. A trade?" she asked. Her voice had a note of doubt in it that hadn't been there before. She wasn't sure of his answer.

Neither was he. He didn't spend much time around other beings, but Maggie was different. She liked the woods, too. And if he didn't help her, she could get hurt or killed out here.

He took her hand and shook it, nodding.

"So, you're going to teach me?" Her smile was so bright it felt like he was standing in a beam of sunlight.

"Mm-hmm." He almost hummed his answer. He'd learned that was easier than trying to talk once his throat got irritated.

"Thank you. That means a lot to—" A bolt of lightning arced down from the sky and slammed into a tree not far from the edge of the clearing.

Thunder boomed and Maggie opened her mouth in a silent scream of fright. Her fingers closed around his hand in a death grip, but she held her ground and didn't let fear overwhelm her.

Fraxx. Standing in the middle of the forest was not a smart place to be during a lightning storm. Especially not the ones on this planet. The storms here were violent, coming on fast and often lasting for hours. He needed to get somewhere safe.

No. He needed to get *them* somewhere safe.

The colony was too far, and he didn't want to deal with the questions they'd face if he appeared with Maggie. There was only one other place to go.

He shoved the box of cookies into her hands. "Hold."

"What was that? Why? Hey!" Maggie protested as he swept her into his arms. A fireman's carry would have been easier for him, but there was no way she'd be able to hold on to the cookies if she were over his shoulders.

He turned and ran.

"What the *fraxx* was that?" she asked again.

"Lightning."

"But the sky was clear!"

"Not for long." His words came out in a rasp and he deactivated his pain receptors. The short-term solution would let him keep talking now and pay for it later.

The wind picked up with every step he took, rattling in the branches and sending the last of the leaves fluttering to the ground.

"This is a storm?"

"A large one," he confirmed. "Your first?"

That won him a tiny smile. "Yup. So, where are we going?"

"Shelter." His voice cracked a little, and she laid a hand on his throat. Her gentle touch felt so good he almost lost his balance and ran them into a tree.

The rain started a few seconds later, a few drops at first, but it wasn't long before the sky went black and the rain became a torrent poured over their heads.

Lightning arced overhead and thunder shook the ground. Maggie trembled in his arms but didn't utter a sound, her hazel eyes locked on the sky.

By the time he reached his cabin, they were both soaked to the skin. He had to set her down to unlatch the door.

"I was expecting a cave. This is much better."

"Cave? No. I'm civilized. Mostly." He stepped aside and swept an arm toward the door in invitation.

It wasn't a large space, but it was everything he needed —warm, dry, and secure. He'd built it himself so he had a comfortable place to sleep those days he didn't feel like going back to town. He might be designed to endure the elements and weather on any world, but that didn't mean he enjoyed it.

Right now it was little more than simple shelter to keep out the wind, rain, and predators, but he had plans. And he wasn't the only one. A few of them were carving their own places out in the wilds. Wreckage and Ruin had a place a few kilometers away, and Axe had claimed a spot for himself by the river. A few Vardarians were setting up out in the woods, too. They were on the other side of the river, but the need for space was the same.

"This is nice," Maggie said.

He tried to ignore how happy her approval made him.

It didn't matter what she thought. This was his place. Made to suit his needs and no one else's, even if she did make the best cookies he'd ever tasted.

Striker's home wasn't like she'd expected. Not that she really thought he lived in a cave. In fact, she'd been expecting something more modern. He was a cyborg after all, and they lived with an alien race that was far more technologically advanced than humans. A log cabin wasn't what she'd envisioned, but that's what it was. Oh, there were modern touches. She'd seen solar panels on the roof and the interior was lit up by light cubes instead of candles, but it was still a cabin made of stacked logs with a door that didn't hang straight.

"You made this place yourself?"

He nodded, shaking himself off before coming inside and shutting the door against the wind and rain. He moved past her to crouch in front of a space heater, activating it with a few quick touches.

While he did that, she set down the box of cookies on a rough-hewn table and started going through her pack. The thermal blanket came out first. She shed her soaked-through jacket and wrapped the blanket around her shoulders to hold on to what body heat she had left.

Fresh socks came next, and she dropped onto a sturdy bench to undo her boots and swap her wet socks for dry ones. She might not have been outside before coming to this planet, but the lower levels of Athens Two were prone to floods and she'd learned early on that a fresh pair of socks made everything seem better.

"How long will this go on?" She pointed at the roof.

He held up two fingers and then added a third.

"Two to three hours? It came out of nowhere."

"Check your comms." His voice was rougher now.

"Stop talking if it hurts. This time, I brought a tablet. We can talk that way."

"Pain blocked."

She'd heard cyborgs could do that. It wasn't a kindness, though. Their creators had given them the ability so they could maintain battle functionality for as long as possible. The idea that he'd do that so he could talk to her… She rose and padded over to him. "Don't do that for me."

He cocked his head and arched one blond brow.

She moved in closer, reaching up to lay her hand over his scarred throat. "I don't like the idea of you hurting later because you talked to me right now. I'm okay. You got me someplace warm and dry. If I had been out there alone, I'd be terrified right now. But I'm here, with you, and I'm not scared."

"Smart person would be." He grinned a little. "Scary cyborg killing machine."

She snorted. "No one who likes cookies as much as you do can be that scary."

He covered her hand with his own. He was warmer than she was, and she leaned in closer without realizing she was doing it until she was pressed up against his broad chest. "My batch-brother gave me this scar. Right before I killed him."

Her first impulse was to pull away, but that was what he wanted. She went with her second thought instead. She rose on her toes and managed to brush a kiss to the tip of his chin. "You had to do it. Didn't you? They made you."

He linked his fingers with hers and slid her hand to the

back of his neck, his gaze locked on hers. "Why aren't you like the others?"

It was hard to think when he was staring at her like that, but she managed to find enough functional brain cells to organize an answer. "You've only known the ones who worked for the corporations. They're assholes. Not all humans are like that. Some of us are awesome."

His full lips quirked up in a lopsided smile. Silken ribbons of desire unfurled inside her, amplifying her attraction and making her shiver in anticipation of the kiss she knew was coming.

It didn't happen.

He moved away from her, letting go of her hand and turning toward the small kitchenette that took up one corner of the cabin. "You're cold. Go sit by the heater. I'll make hot drinks. Do you want *ja'kreesh* or coffee?"

What she'd like was for him to come back and kiss her, but apparently that wasn't going to happen. She buried her disappointment and moved closer to the heater. "You shouldn't be talking so much."

He looked up in surprise. Had he not realized how much he was talking? It wasn't a kiss... but it was progress.

"*Ja'kreesh* is that Torski jet fuel I've heard about. Right? Do you think it's safe for me to try it?"

He considered and then nodded as he held up his thumb and forefinger about an inch apart.

"That sounds good. Thank you." She gestured around them. "It would seem you rescued me again. I... I'm not used to anyone doing that for me. Jade did, but she's gone and I don't know how the *fraxx* to find her."

She hadn't meant to talk about any of it, but once the words started, they came in a flood she couldn't stop. She told him how much she missed her friend and how worried she was. She left out the details of what Jade had been doing and why, but the rest was more of the truth than she'd told anyone in a long time.

Striker brought her a towel, made her tea, and listened. He didn't interrupt or try to tell her what to do next. He just nodded and made the right noises every time she paused.

By the time she'd finished sharing, she was warm enough to leave the heater and move to the table. He set down a steel mug half full of something dark and steaming in front of her and then took a seat across from her.

"Drink slowly," he said.

"No talking. And thank you." She pulled out the tablet she'd brought and set it down between them as a reminder they had another way to communicate.

"How about this instead?" His voice, or something close to it, was coming through the tablet now.

"How the *fraxx* are you doing that?" She'd thought he could type on it, not project his voice.

"Cyborg, remember?" He tapped his temple. "I was designed for tactical infiltration. That includes accessing other battle groups' tech and communications channels."

It was weird to hold a conversation with someone this way. Striker wasn't actually talking. His mouth didn't move, and the voice coming from the tablet speaker was flat and toneless. It was him, though. And this was better than him trying to talk and hurting himself.

She'd looked up a number of sign languages since their first meeting, but she didn't know which one he used. "Your signs. Which language are they? I looked, but there are so many."

"My own. This happened while I was a prisoner. They deactivated our internal comm channels, so I had to come up with another way to communicate."

Well, *fraxx*. So much for teaching herself.

"Why do you ask?"

"I thought…" She took a sip of her drink to buy herself more time. The flavor was nutty and smooth.

"This is delicious!" She took a bigger drink.

Striker raised a hand in warning. "Slow! You're going to feel it when that hits your system in a few minutes. And I want to know what you were about to say."

"I thought I could try to learn sign language. So I could understand you. I guess that doesn't matter so much now that I know we can talk like this."

"Why?"

And wasn't that a loaded question? She couldn't tell him she thought about him all the time. Or that he was featured in some very x-rated dreams. She'd already baked him cookies and arranged for weekly deliveries of the same. If she said anything more, she might as well put out a flashing holo-sign confessing she had a crush on him.

"I wanted to learn it because I didn't like the idea of you being on your own out here with no one to talk to. I forgot about your internal comms. You can talk to the other cyborgs any time you want. Can't you?"

He nodded, and she ducked her head to hide her flushed cheeks. Idiot. He wasn't alone at all. He didn't need her company.

"What's wrong?"

She downed another mouthful of the warm drink without thinking. "Nothing's wrong. I just… whoa."

It was like someone had attached a booster rocket to

her energy levels. She was suddenly alert and ready to take on the world.

"And that's enough of that for you. Your heart rate just went through the stratosphere." Striker moved her mug to his side of the table, out of easy reach.

"I'm fine." She held out her hand to prove her point and then frowned when she noticed her fingers were shaking. "Or maybe I should eat something to soak up that rocket fuel I drank."

"You haven't eaten lately?"

"I was busy making cookies and forgot to have lunch."

Striker got to his feet and went back to the kitchenette, pulling open cupboards and taking down various boxes and containers. Within minutes, a pile of food was heaped onto the table in front of her. Crackers, food tabs, dried fruit and trail bars.

"Eat."

"Anyone ever mention you're kind of bossy?"

"All part of my charm. And part of my programming. I was the leader of my unit."

"That explains a lot." She'd been learning about the way cyborg units were made. They were usually composed of batch-siblings, genetically linked cyborgs created with complementary skill sets and behavior programming. They were even brought online at the same time.

"You don't like bossy men?" His expression stayed as neutral as his synthesized voice.

She had no clue how to answer the question. If she said she didn't, would he be insulted? If she said she did, would he start telling her what to do all the time? "Not usually. I find that most guys who like to give orders expect everyone around them to obey without question, and they like to punish anyone who thinks for themselves."

"Punish? Who did it? Someone here?" He was at her side so quickly she barely saw him move, his hand slamming down on the table beside her with enough force to rattle their mugs.

"Here? No. Before. Back on Earth." She set her hand on his to try and calm him.

"No one will hurt you here. I won't let them."

She squeezed his hand. "And you're going to teach me how to protect myself."

"Yes." He spoke this time, his voice so rough now it was barely more than a growl.

A thrill of desire danced down her spine. Bossy or not, Striker was sexy when he was riled. She liked it more than she wanted to admit. "I don't like bossy men, but you're not like the others I've known. You're different."

"You have no idea." He flashed her a smile that should have scared her half to death. All it did was make her heart beat a tattoo against her ribs. Or maybe that was the *ja'kreesh*.

She knew it wasn't. It was him, and she was in so much trouble.

5

ONCE THE *JA'KREESH* hit her bloodstream, Maggie didn't stop talking. The constant chatter should have made Striker crazy, but he discovered he really didn't mind. In fact, it was a nice change from the silence he usually lived with.

She talked openly about any subject he asked her about. Not that she told him everything, but he didn't expect her to. He'd already gleaned enough to realize that whatever Maggie had been back on Earth, she was trying to put that part of her life behind her. That was the only thing everyone in Haven had in common. They were all looking for a fresh start at a new life.

The storm behaved differently than the others he'd experienced. The thunder and lightning ended quickly, but the wind and rain intensified. Maggie got several concerned messages asking where she was and if she needed help. She gave them all the same answer. She was hunkered down somewhere safe and would be back when the storm ended. She never mentioned where, or who she was with. His little human was protecting him.

Not that she was *his* anything. And he certainly didn't need her protection. *She* needed his.

"*How's the cabin?*" Edge's voice sounded inside his head.

"*Dry and snug. I need a bigger heater, though. This place is going to get cold when winter hits.*"

"*Or you could stay in your big, comfy home in town,*" Edge said.

"*I like having options. There a reason you're checking in on me?*"

"*Skye is worried about one of her humans. Apparently she likes to go for long walks in the woods and got caught out in the storm. Skye wants me to organize a group to go look for her before night falls. I know you're not a fan of the humans being here, but we could use your help to find her.*"

Fraxx. So much for secrets.

"*No need to send out a search party. I already know where she is.*"

After a long, pregnant pause Edge asked, "*And where is that?*"

"*Maggie is currently bouncing off the walls of my cabin. I may have given her a little ja'kreesh to warm her up. Humans really don't handle that stuff very well.*"

"*Maggie Piper, a human, is in your cabin. Your cabin that I have yet to be invited to visit.*"

"*If I had left her outside, she'd have gotten hurt or killed. I was protecting the colony's interests. Do me a favor, though. Don't tell Skye where she is. Just tell her I'll get Maggie back before dinner. Apparently they're having something called macaroni and cheese and Maggie doesn't want to miss it.*"

"*Did you get hit by lightning while you were out there? Maybe take a branch to the head?*"

"*Asshole.*"

"And there's the Striker I know. I was worried for a second there."

"I'm fine. Maggie will be back soon. She's... not so bad. For a human."

"Uh huh. I'm going to need to meet this paragon of her kind at some point. That's high praise coming from you."

"Did I mention you're an asshole? I need to get back to Maggie. She's telling me about what her life on Earth was like. Did you know they actually eat *the mold that grows inside the air recyclers?"*

"That's disgusting. Go. Talk to your human. I'll deal with Skye."

Striker brought his full attention back to Maggie. She'd gone quiet. A quick replay of his audio told him she'd stopped about ten seconds ago. "Sorry. That was Edge. Skye was trying to organize a search party to find you and bring you home. He wanted me to join in."

"I told her I was fine!" Maggie was indignant.

"She worries." And he knew why. Skye had been created after the Resource Wars, and her behavioral programming wasn't standard. The lab rats at Reamus had done something to her and a handful of other female cyborgs, turning them into den mothers who spent most of their time taking care of the others. They were still combat capable, but they were generally calmer and less aggressive. They kept the peace, treated minor injuries, and made life easier for both captives and captors.

"So, they know where I am?"

"Edge does. All Skye knows is that you're safe and I'll have you back for dinner."

"Do you really think she's going to be satisfied with that?"

He made a wry face. "Probably not."

Maggie's comms chimed. "Guess who that is."

"Busted," he said and then gestured for her to answer it.

Maggie pasted a bright smile on her face and opened a video channel instead of replying by text this time. "Hi, Skye."

"Where the hell are you?"

"The same place I was the last time you asked. Safe and sound."

"You're with Striker. That's... not what I'd call safe."

"He can hear you."

"Oh good, that will save me repeating myself later. Striker, if anything happens to Maggie, I will kick your ass so hard you'll reach high orbit."

Maggie turned her screen so he could see it. "He's not going to hurt me! I gave him cookies. It's all fine."

Skye pinched the bridge of her nose. "You gave him the cookies you made? Wait. That's why you took them into the forest? They were for *him*?"

"Uh. Yeah. He saved me from a bark spider the other day, and I wanted to thank him."

"You do realize that when I warned you there were dangerous cyborgs in the woods, he's the one I was talking about. Right? And what the *fraxx* is a bark spider?"

He'd heard enough. He stepped into view and made an obscene gesture at Skye with both hands. "She'll be home by dinner." Then he exerted enough control over Maggie's comm unit to end the call.

"Did you hang up on her? You are a braver man than I am."

He nodded brusquely and then went back to his seat. He'd deal with Skye later. It didn't sit well that she was warning the humans he was dangerous. He didn't want to hurt anyone. He just wanted to be left the *fraxx* alone.

"You're upset." Maggie snagged a cookie out of the box and then bounded off the bench to offer it to him. "This will help. Chocolate helps everything."

"Not upset," he told her through the tablet. "Annoyed."

"Because Skye warned me about you? She never said your name, you know. She just told me some of your kind were out in the woods and preferred to be left alone."

"I do prefer to be alone, but she doesn't need to worry about me or the others. I'll talk to them. Let them know about you."

"What are their names?"

"You want to know their names? Are you going to bring them cookies, too?" He was not jealous. Nope. Not.

"Would it bother you if I did?" she asked. She was bouncing on the balls of her feet, the stimulant making it impossible for her to stay still.

He shrugged. *Definitely not jealous.*

"I just want to know their names, so I know who to call out to if I see them around. No cookies will be involved."

"You'll only see Axe if you follow the river toward the ocean. You're more likely run into Wreckage and Ruin out here. They've got a place a few klicks from here." He pointed in the general direction of their cabin.

"And where is *here*?"

Ah. Right. Human. She had no onboard navigational software or positional data. "Can't your comm unit tell you that information?"

"No. I went with the basic model. No tracking data. Unless I set off the emergency beacon, no one can find me... or my caches."

He sent a data file to her tablet with a thought. "Coordinates to this place are now on your tablet. If you get caught in another storm, you can come here."

"And what if I want to see you?"

He planned to tell her the same thing he told everyone else. If he wanted company, he'd let them know. What came out of his mouth was something entirely different. "Then send me a message. If I'm around, I'll meet you."

Her eyes widened and her lush lips turned up in a smile. "Yeah?"

"Yeah. We can train here, too."

She gave a little whoop of joy and then stunned him by throwing her arms around his neck and hugging him. "Thank you!"

She was soft, warm, and smelled like rainwater and flowers. Her breath fanned across the skin of his neck, and when she brushed her lips against his throat, he almost forgot to breathe.

The things this little human made him feel…

She withdrew a second later, her eyes dancing with mischief. She knew the effect she'd had on him. He was tempted to haul her into his lap and teach her what happened to those who played with fire.

"Cookie?" She offered him one of the treats. He took it and then broke it in two, handing half back to her.

"Eat. Then we're heading back. I promised to have you home by dinner."

"I'm going to get drenched again. Aren't I?" she asked, resignedly.

"We'll figure something out." He didn't want her getting cold and wet again. Humans were delicate and susceptible to chills and other ailments. He needed to get Maggie back to the colony without risking her health.

"This training we're going to do. What do I need to bring?"

The question caught him off guard. "Do you have a weapon?"

"Not yet. I'm learning how to fire a blaster, though."

"Then don't worry about it. I'll bring what you need to get started." He already had something in mind. He'd come up with the idea the last time he'd visited Damos and Tra'var, and the prototype should be ready soon. If it worked, he'd have them make another one the right size for Maggie. Once she was armed and trained, she'd be able to protect herself and the colony. If she was going to stay here, she'd have to learn how to fight to defend her home from anyone who threatened to take what they were building here. Someone would. He knew that. It was only a matter of time.

Maggie knew it wasn't possible, but it was as if Striker moved so fast on the way back that he actually dodged the raindrops. She was still relatively dry when he set her down outside the door to the main hall.

"Thank you." She thought about hugging him, but she didn't want anyone to see them together until she was ready to explain things, so instead, she held out her hand to him.

He took it, caressing the back of her hand with his thumb for a brief moment.

When the door opened this time, she didn't look away. Even so, she only caught a flicker of motion before Striker was gone and she was left holding her hand out to empty air.

"Maggie!" Skye grabbed her by the shoulders and pulled her inside. "Are you okay?"

"I'm fine. Or I will be once you release your death grip."

"Oops. Sorry." Skye let go and then moved past her to check outside.

"He's gone," she told the cyborg woman.

"He'd better be. If I see him, I'm going to want a word."

Maggie tapped her temple. "Can't you just talk to him on your snazzy internal channels?"

"Nope. He's blocking me." Skye closed the door with more force than it needed and then spun around to glower at her. "How long has this thing with Striker been going on?"

"There is no *thing*. That day you and I talked by the woods, I nearly got bitten by a big, nasty bug. Striker killed it and taught me how to spot them. That's it."

"You left out the bit about you bringing him cookies and that he took you to his place. Do you realize most of us don't even know where it is? He doesn't like visitors. Or most beings. Especially not human ones."

"I think he likes me, or maybe he just likes cookies. Have you ever tried *ja'kreesh*? I like it. How come we don't have any in our stores? Oh, he's going to teach me to protect myself. So I guess he must like me enough to help me stay alive. I don't think he's so bad. A little grumpy. And what's up with his throat? Why hasn't anyone helped him get better?"

Skye blinked at her. "Holy *fraxx*. How much *ja'kreesh* did he give you?"

"Not much. And he did warn me to drink it slowly. I might not have listened."

"You not listening does not surprise me. The fact he didn't kill you does. He *must* like you." Skye shook her head. "I will never understand males."

"I think I'm insulted."

"What? Oh, no. Not that he likes you. That he likes anyone. Striker is…"

Maggie lowered her voice. "He's damaged? Carries a lot of resentment and anger about what was done to him. Blames himself for having to kill his own?"

"Oh wow. He told you about that? He doesn't talk about Reamus. At all. Ever. Not even to those of us who were there with him."

"He talks to me about it."

Skye gave her an odd look. "This conversation is going to require alcohol."

"It is?"

"Oh, yes. It is. Come with me."

"But dinner?"

"Trust me, we're going somewhere with much better food. Don't tell anyone I said that, though." Skye raised her voice. "I need to debrief Maggie about what happened. I'm taking her back to her habi-pod. We'll manage dinner on our own."

"You got it," Shadow called back.

Several of the other human women looked at Maggie with curiosity. She raised her hands in a shrug. That was all she had time for. A second later Skye had her by the hand and was pulling her toward the door.

"Come on. Let's get you cleaned up."

"Do I get to know where we're really going?" Maggie asked in a soft tone.

Skye didn't answer until they were outside and jogging through the rain. "The Bar None."

"But that's on the other side of the river. I'm not supposed to go there, yet."

"Technically it's on the bridge in the middle of the river, and at this point, I'm not worried about you running into your mates. You're ready."

"I am?"

"Close enough. Besides, there's someone I think you should meet."

"Who? Where? Why? Do they have *ja'kreesh*? I could use a little more of that."

"Her name is Anya. She runs the Bar None, and given your skill set, I thought you might want to check out her establishment and see if you'd want to work there. And while she does serve that Torski rocket fuel, you are not having anymore. Not if you want sleep sometime in the next few days."

"Days?" no one had mentioned how long the effects lasted.

"Days. At least that's what I've heard. A mug of that stuff can keep a full-grown Torski on their feet all day. Imagine what it can do for species not half that size."

"Oops."

"You'll be fine. You're just not likely to sleep tonight."

"I've slept more since leaving Earth than I have in years. I can afford to skip a night."

"Yeah. I sleep better since coming here, too."

They didn't say anything more. The peaceful silence continued after they reached Maggie's pod. She washed up, combed the tangles out of her hair, and changed into fresh clothes. She picked one of the tops she'd worn at her old job, a dark green blouse that showed just enough cleavage to increase her tips.

"This work?"

"You clean up nicely." Skye grinned and tossed her jacket over. "Come on. I messaged Anya while you were dressing. This weather is keeping everyone at home. The place is quiet and currently no unmated Vardarian males are around to complicate things."

"Good." She'd come here with the understanding that she might end up mated to a pair of aliens. When they sensed their *mahaya*, pheromones took over from logic and things happened fast. She'd been fine with it. But now, things were different. She didn't want to be bound to a couple of strangers. She wanted… oh holy *fraxx*. No.

Striker was hot as hell, sure. But he was also growly, grumpy, and bossy. And she barely knew him. And she had no idea if he liked her. And this was only a crush. Right? She was infatuated with the man who had saved her life. That was totally normal. That's all this was.

"You okay?"

"Yeah. Just getting my head sorted. It's a little hard to focus right now."

"I bet. Ready to face the rain again?"

"If there's a drink at the end of it? Hell yes." She hadn't had a drink since leaving Earth. But tonight, it felt like she had something to celebrate.

Their destination was the only human-owned business in the colony. She'd heard that the owner was a friend of Phaedra's. She'd met the pink-haired cyber-jockey turned Vardarian princess a few times and liked her. In fact, she suspected she and Jade probably knew each other, but she hadn't figured out how to mention it without being overheard. She wasn't sure Phaedra's mates would appreciate anyone mentioning their *mahaya* had a shady past, and one of them was always within earshot.

The bridge was wide enough to allow traffic to flow in

both directions and still have room for buildings and a marketplace. Tonight, the market was shut down, the stalls emptied and secured against the foul weather. Some businesses were still open, though, and the Bar None remained well-lit and welcoming.

They made their way inside, and Maggie assessed the place with the practiced eye of someone who knew the trade. Anya's design was ideal. Plenty of space with the tables placed to allow staff and bots to move around easily. The furniture was of the same sturdy, mass-produced kind she'd seen in every establishment she'd worked in—easy to clean and cheap to replace.

The tables had electronic menus that sent their orders straight to the kitchen or bar. She could hear voices from the kitchen, so that was staffed by living beings, but the bar was manned by several servo-droids, all of which were currently offline.

"*Fraxxing* pieces of crap!" a woman swore as they stripped off their dripping coats.

"And hello to you, too. Anya. Those droids malfunctioning again?"

A woman in her mid-forties popped up from behind the counter and flashed them a grin. "Hi, Skye. Oh! This was why you asked about who was in the bar tonight. You've brought one of the new arrivals!"

"Anya, this is Maggie. Maggie, Anya Hutchinson."

"It's a pleasure to meet you. I like your place. Great vibe. What's up with the droids?" Maggie asked the auburn-haired woman without pausing for breath. Yeah. No more *ja'kreesh* for her.

"She paid rock-bottom prices and got rock-bottom quality. I warned you not to trust that dealer. You should have gone with Kirk." Another woman's voice came from the back corner of the room.

Maggie could only make out a few details. Flight suit. Ample curves. Fair hair cut short.

"Kirk couldn't guarantee delivery for months," Anya retorted in a tone that made it clear they'd had this conversation before.

"But his stuff would work," the other woman replied.

"Quit being a pain in my ass or I'll have to point out you haven't paid your tab this week."

"No need to get huffy." The woman stood and walked out of the shadow. She was older, with silver hair and lines around her eyes and mouth that deepened when she smiled. "I'm Hezza B, by the way. Nice to meet you both."

"I didn't know there was another human here," Skye said, walking over, hand outstretched in greeting.

"Me? I'm just visiting. I'm a trader and an old friend of Anya's."

Skye looked at Hezza and then at Anya. "You're related."

Anya laughed. "Told you they'd notice."

"And yet you're not so smart as to listen to your mother when she tells you not to buy crap from shifty characters like Vellar."

Mother? Maggie looked at the two of them more closely. There was some resemblance, but it wasn't marked. "Nice to meet you, Hezza."

"Same. I got here yesterday. Brought some stuff I thought you Earth girls might like. I can bring it by tomorrow if you're interested? I was told you lot weren't allowed over the bridge yet." Hezza grinned. "You escaping early?"

"Special circumstances. I needed a drink," Skye said and dropped into a nearby chair.

"Droids are out of commission, but I can still remember how to make a cocktail," Anya said.

"Or you could get Maggie to make it. She's a bartender," Skye said.

"Really? How much experience do you have?"

"A decade and change. Granted, most of what I know are Earth drinks, but I scored some gigs in the upper sectors where the visitors would stay. I know a few of the more popular off-world drinks, too." Maggie gestured to the droids. "And I know a few things about repairing busted bar droids."

"Can I keep her?" Anya asked Skye? "Please? Free drinks for a month if you let me keep her."

"You don't want to test me first?" Maggie wasn't sure why she was asking. She should shut up and take the job. Maybe *ja'kreesh* had a downside after all. Words were coming out of her mouth before she had time to vet them.

"Test. Right. I should do that. How about you make us this round? I'll have a Martian Martini," Anya said.

"Whiskey with a twist," Hezza said.

"Paralyzer," Skye said.

"Vodka or tequila?" Maggie asked automatically.

"Oh, bonus points already." Anya grinned and pointed to the bar. "Go forth and make the drinks, and one for yourself, of course."

"Not *ja'kreesh*!" Skye called after her as she bounced over to the bar.

"I have no idea how to brew that, so no problem."

It didn't take her long to find everything. Droids kept everything in a specific order, and all she needed to do was figure out which program they were running. She made everyone's drinks and delivered them before going back to pour herself a beer. "You have stout? Is this the real thing?"

"It is," Anya confirmed.

"Skye, can she keep me? Please? I haven't seen a bar this well-stocked in… ever. And clean! This is bartender heaven."

"Yes, she can keep you. I ran the idea by Shadow while you were making drinks. Congratulations, you are now officially graduated. Welcome to Haven colony."

They raised their glasses in toast as she joined them, elated and a little stunned.

"I'm done? That's it?"

"You should keep attending the classes, and it will take a few days for us to figure out where you'll be moving to, but yes. You're done. This isn't really a regimented plan. The goal is to get you all integrated with the colony once you're settled. I think today proves you're ready."

"What happened today?" Hezza asked.

Skye explained, with Maggie jumping in to add details along the way.

"Striker? I don't think I've met him yet," Anya said when they were done.

"Probably not. He's not very social. He goes running with Denz and Edge a few mornings a week, though. You might have seen him. Big. Blond. Doesn't talk."

Anya grimaced. "Ugh, no. That would involve two things I don't do. Cardio and mornings."

"Three. You don't do blonds, either. Not since… what was his name?" Hezza teased her daughter.

This time Anya's face twisted into one of pure horror. "Do not say his name. If we say it, he'll appear and ask me for money again. Besides, there have been blonds since then. I just don't introduce them all to you. They tend to stick around longer that way."

"This is… not how I imagined someone would talk to their parent," Skye said, her words muffled by her glass.

"You've never seen… oh! Of course not." Anya laid a friendly hand on the cyborg's arm. "Sorry."

"Adult relationships between parent and kids can be complicated. Which is why I haven't spoken to my mother in years. She doesn't know I'm here," Maggie said.

Skye looked bewildered. "You didn't tell her? But she's your *mother*."

"Complicated, remember? Also, we don't like each other. Love, sure. Like? Not even a little."

"See?" Anya said to her mother. "We're not so bad, you and I. Not only do you know where I am, but I got you an invite to trade here." Then Anya raised her glass again. "To family. The ones we're tied to, and the ones we make for ourselves."

Maggie happily drank to that, savoring the rich taste of the dark beer she'd poured for herself. Jade had been the family she'd chosen for herself. Now she was a full member of the colony, she'd have more ways to find out what happened to her. This had been their dream, and she wanted Jade to be here to enjoy it with her. She wanted to share everything about this new world. Well, almost everything. Striker she'd keep to herself. Jade could find her own guy… just as soon as she got here.

6

___

STRIKER HADN'T CARRIED a comm unit since the wars ended. There'd been no need until now. The few times he'd needed to talk to one of the non-cyborg colonists he'd used the system in his home. Now, he needed to have his comms with him in case Maggie wanted to talk to him.

She did. Several times a day for the last two days. First to set up a time for their first lesson, and after that there had been a steady flow of text messages and occasional vid recordings. She never tried to talk to him directly, which he appreciated. But she'd leave him messages and send him notes about her day.

He hadn't realized how many classes she attended: languages and cultures, life skills like cooking, and basic maintenance. Energy weapons training had been added recently. No wonder she only came to the woods every few days.

His comm chimed again as he made his way through the back alleys of the artists' quarter. Maggie wanted to know if he liked something called a walnut. He had no idea what that was, but he was willing to try anything she made him. He sent her a quick text back telling her so.

Murals decorated the walls in this area, and hints to the various types of artisans at work lay piled up by gates and back doors. Broken pottery shards, wood shavings, and piles of metal waited to be forged into something new.

The steady ring of hammers told him the males he wanted to see were hard at work despite the cold, rainy weather. Given their vocation, they were probably happy the heat of summer was over.

The gate swung open at a touch, and he stepped through into the walled yard. The space was partially covered by an overhang that protected the occupants from the worst of the weather. Both males were working at the forge today, their hammers falling in a pattern of blows that was almost musical.

They both looked up at the same time. "I thought we'd see you today," Tra'var greeted him in Vardarian, and then switched to Galactic Standard. "And before you ask, yes, it's ready."

"And I think you're going to start a new trend. I can't believe none of us thought of this before." Damos set down his hammer and placed the piece they'd been working on back in the forge before coming out to meet him.

"Traditional thinking is hard to break out of," Tra'v agreed.

Physically, the two were as different as night and day. Tra'var was tall and blond, with silver skin and blue eyes ringed in black. Damos was short for a Vardarian, with a much heavier build than his *anrik*. He had golden skin and pale amber eyes that reminded Striker of pictures he'd seen of the wolves that once roamed Earth.

But while they differed physically, they were alike in many other ways. They were both masters of their craft, passionate about their work and dedicated to spending their lives trying to come up with new ways to annoy and insult each other. They reminded him of the way he and his batch-siblings used to bicker with each other. Only Tra'v and Damos weren't related by genetics. They were blood-brothers, bound to each other for life by ceremony rather than biology.

"Show me." His voice was rusty, but not as bad as he'd expected. He hadn't spoken aloud since that day with Maggie, and the rest must have been enough to undo the damage.

"It's just inside. I'll get it," Damos offered. He walked past Striker, who did his best not to look at the other male's wings. Something about them didn't look quite right, like they were slightly too small for Damos's heavy build. Or maybe it was fine, and he was imagining things. Physical flaws weren't something Striker had much experience with. If a cyborg was too badly damage, they were terminated. As far as he knew, he was the most damaged one to ever avoid that fate. Sometimes, he wished they hadn't done him that courtesy.

"I'll need a dagger, too."

"Another one?" Tra'var asked. "You lose yours?"

"Smaller. For a human female."

"A gift?" Tra'v beamed. "For a human female? What's her name?"

"Maggie."

"She's your mate, then?" the Vardarian asked casually.

"What? *Fraxx*, no! She's a… a friend."

"That you're buying a blade for. In our culture, that's a serious declaration of intent."

"He's buying a blade for a female? I swear the *sharhal* is contagious. Even the cyborgs are catching it now." Damos returned, holding a length of black metal in one large hand.

"No mating fever. No mating involved at all. She hired me."

"Uh, to do what?" Tra'v asked, confused.

"Self-defense." The real answer was longer and would only lead to more questions.

"I thought the humans didn't have much in the way of currency. What's she paying you with?" Damos asked.

"Cookies."

Both males stared at him.

"She made me cookies. Chocolate ones. They're really good."

"This is starting to sound like a mating thing again," Tra'var said.

"It is *not*."

Both males held up their hands. "As you say, my friend. Enough talk of females. Let's discuss something more interesting. Weapons." Damos held out the black metal shaft to Striker. "Your *kes'tarv*."

He took it, testing the weight and balance of the shaft. "Lighter than I expected."

"Turns out, most of the weight in a blaster is in the casing. It was a surprisingly easy alteration," Tra'var explained.

He gripped the shaft in both hands and twisted. Both ends extended and locked into place, leaving him holding more than a meter of steel not much thicker than his thumb. "How?" he asked.

"We wanted to make sure you couldn't discharge it accidentally. There's a notch in the handle. If you press it twice, you'll be able to fire as a stun bolt. Three and you're going to fry whatever you're shooting at," Tra'var said.

He nodded. "How do I know which end to aim at the target?"

"We set the trigger mechanism so it's closer to the shooter than the target, just like a pulse rifle."

"And I added a visual cue." Damos pointed to a ring of silver metal on one end. "Silver toward whatever you're aiming at."

"That works. I'd never hear the end of it if I shot myself with my own weapon." They'd done amazing work and deserved to hear him say it. "This is incredible."

"We'd like to sell more of them. But it's your design, so..." Tra'v trailed off and they both looked at him expectantly.

"Of course."

They beamed. "Excellent. We talked about it. Since this was your idea, we'd like to cut you in on a portion of the profits. Say, ten percent?" Tra'v said.

"No money. Your work. You keep it."

That made them both frown. "Then you're getting that one for free," Damos said.

Striker nodded and then held up two fingers.

"You want us to make you another one?"

"Smaller. Human sized."

Neither male laughed, but their eyes were dancing with barely hidden humor. "For your *friend*?"

"Yes."

"No problem. We've got some made for youths. In fact, I bet we can find a blade for your friend in that size, too. The knife you can have today. The *kes'tarv*..." Tra'v looked at Damos. "Three days?"

"Four. Will take me a while to get the balance right on a smaller version."

"That's fine. I'd like it to have a tracker of some kind, too. Simple. No satellite link." He wanted to be able to find her if she got lost or ran into trouble.

"You going to start her with a practice one? We've got a few used ones in stock."

Striker shook his head and collapsed the *kes'tarv*, hanging it on his belt. "Metal later. For now, wood."

"Old school training," Damos said approvingly.

"Wood breaks," Tra'v muttered. "Metal doesn't."

Striker grinned. "Exactly. Eventually I'll be her practice dummy."

"Definitely wood, then." Tra'var said.

"You're buying her weapons and letting her use them on you. She must make the best cookies in the galaxy," Damos said. "Come on inside. We'll find a blade for your little baker."

Striker ignored the good-humored teasing and followed them inside. He wasn't doing this because of Maggie's baking. He was doing it because she needed someone to show her how to survive in this place, and he was qualified to do it.

Maggie shoved her hands a little deeper into her pockets and tried to ignore the nip in the air. Cold wasn't something she was used to experiencing. Hive cities were exactly what their name suggested—crowded places full of warm bodies. Getting rid of waste heat was a constant challenge, especially on the lower levels.

"I'll get used to it," she reminded herself as she

walked, her breath condensing into a temporary cloud as her words hit the air. There was a lot to get used to these days. The gravity. The weather. New foods and languages. And now she was learning how to mix drinks she could barely pronounce with liquors she'd never heard of before.

It was tiring, challenging, and wonderful. Anya was a rare kind of boss, the sort that folded her employees into her family and made sure everyone felt welcome. The kitchen staff turned out to be a trio of mated Vardarians who worked together with the seamless flow of long practice. They laughed and fought and cooked some of the best meals Maggie had ever tasted.

She'd shared her cookie recipe with them, too, and they'd transformed it into a new dessert. She had no idea what they'd done, but her simple recipe had been combined with something similar to ice cream and a booze-infused fruit sauce that elevated the simple cookie into something close to divinity.

The coordinates to Striker's place were in her tablet, but the damned thing was glitching. Or maybe she'd messed up linking it to her new comm unit. This one actually had positioning software so she could figure out where she was and how to get to Striker's home. Hezza had sold it to her, giving her a fair deal and showing her how to turn the tracking system off and on so she'd only show up when she wanted to. She liked Hezza. The woman was grounded and infinitely practical, but she'd somehow avoided becoming cynical despite the life she'd led. Neither she nor Anya said it outright, but it was easy enough to tell that Hezza did whatever was needed to get by, and that meant bending or breaking more than a few laws along the way. The older trader had promised to try and dig up whatever information she could about Jade, too. It was a longshot, but she appreciated the offer.

Maggie hadn't opened up about her life on Earth yet, but she got the sense that Anya and her mother had already guessed her hands weren't entirely clean either.

"Dammit. I should be there by now," she muttered and smacked the edge of the tablet. The dot that represented her hadn't moved in the last few minutes. The thing was definitely malfunctioning. Maybe Striker could figure out what was wrong with it… if she ever found him.

She put the tablet away and sent him a message instead. "Can't find your place. Positioning software screwed up. Your cookies and I need an escort." Once that was sent, she held up her comm unit and took a quick video of the surrounding area and then sent that, too. Maybe it would help him figure out where the hell she was.

He answered her only a few seconds later. "On my way. Start singing. I'll find you."

Veth. He'd heard her singing to herself. That was embarrassing. She couldn't carry a tune to save her life, but that didn't stop her from enjoying it… when she was alone.

She started humming and then broke into full-throated song, stringing lyrics together as she carefully checked the tree behind her for anything alive before leaning against it.

About five minutes later she heard a triple-knock, like something rapping against a tree trunk. She banged her stick against the tree in response, sending a shower of water droplets cascading down on her head from an earlier rain shower.

"There are times the outdoors really sucks vacuum," she grumbled and pulled up her hood.

The knocks came several more times, each one closer. She kept singing and rapping on her tree. Before long, she heard a noise in the brush and Striker stepped into view. He was wearing dark green and gray today, a mottled pattern that helped him blend into the woods. He held a metal staff in one hand, but then he touched it with both hands and it contracted to a bit of metal less than a third its full length.

Unlike her, he'd been smart enough to wear his hood up, and he swept it back as he approached, revealing his handsome face.

Damn. The man really was as good looking as she'd remembered. He'd shaved recently, though his jaw was already shadowed by stubble. "Hi. Thanks for the rescue."

He cocked a brow and lifted one hand.

"I don't know what happened. The program is glitchy. It stopped working and once that happened, I stayed put and called you."

"Smart." He spoke the single word aloud.

She pulled the tablet out of the pack and showed it to him. "See?"

For a moment they stood in silence as he tapped the screen, his frown deepening every few seconds.

"It's not the tablet. The program seems fine. Might be a solar storm affecting the satellites." His voice came through the speaker this time.

"Yeah. That used to happen on Earth a lot, too. Someone needs to start making maps that won't fail every time there's a solar flare."

"Interesting notion. You volunteering?"

"Maybe. First, I need to learn how to stay alive out here. Then we'll talk map making." She beamed. "And I'll need to find time in my busy schedule. I'm a working woman now." She hadn't told him about the new job in her messages. She'd wanted to share that in person.

"You are? Since when? I thought the new arrivals weren't due to join the rest of the colony for weeks yet."

"Skye and Shadow decided to make an exception for me. I'm working at the Bar None, and eventually I'll be moving to the other side of the river. It'll take me a little longer to get to our training sessions once that happens, but they're going to let me pick where I want to live." She still couldn't wrap her mind around the idea of having her own place. Hers. Not a rental. Not a by-the-day rented pod. A home. One she could choose for herself.

"You might like to check out the artists' quarter. It's noisier than some, but the beings there are friendly, interesting, and you'll never be bored. There's always something to look at and someone to talk to."

"You like it there? Somehow I didn't think you spent much time in Haven."

He held up the metal rod and then slipped into a loop on his belt. "They sell some intriguing things."

"What is that, exactly?"

"A *kes'tarv*. A traditional Vardarian weapon. Not standard gear, but you'll see them if you go to the training arenas."

"It's perfect for what I'd need." She hefted her walking stick. "Better than this thing. What does one of those cost?" She needed to buy furniture first, but food and clothing were cheap and plentiful. Between work and her scavenging, she could probably afford one in a few months. Less if she could buy a cheap, mass-created version.

"First, you need to learn how to use one. Then we'll talk price."

Elation filled her. "You're going to teach me how to use *that*?"

"I am."

"Thank you! I can use it to keep away rockclaws, kill bark spiders, and poke anyone who gets too handsy on the job."

His expression turned stormy. "Who touched you?"

"It's part of the job. I'm used to it. Males of any species are all the same. The more they drink, the more they flirt. It's fine."

"It is not." He didn't use the tablet this time, and his voice was pure growl. "Names."

"I don't know their names. I didn't ask. A few Vardarians have gotten flirty, and a couple of the cyborgs, too. That's all. I've dealt with a lot worse."

"Vardarians shouldn't be flirting unless you are their mate."

She laughed. "They're not celibate before they find their mate. It's just no-strings-attached sex. And cyborgs aren't monks, either. Not even close. By the end of my first shift, I had a much better understanding of why they were giving us a chance to adjust before introducing us to the rest of the colony. It would be easy to get overwhelmed."

He growled and pointed back the way he'd come. "Then we better get started on your training. Come."

7

THE LAST TIME she'd been to his place it had been pouring rain and miserable. She'd barely noticed anything about it. This time, she took a better look. A lean-to type shed at the back of the cabin housed unused building materials and a variety of tools. The batteries for the solar array were stored there, too. A small clearing lay beyond it with a couple of rough-hewn logs laid out around a firepit.

"I bet this place is beautiful in the summer. Do you come out here to stare at the stars?"

"I've seen enough of the stars to last a lifetime. I like to watch the flames and listen to the night."

"Did you know I had never seen stars until I left Earth? I don't know if I'll ever get tired of looking at them."

"We've lived very different lives."

Something lay in his tone, a hardness that hadn't been there before, but when she looked at him, he didn't seem angry. He was using the tablet again, so maybe it was distortion from the speaker.

"We have. But that just means we've got different stories to tell." One day, she wanted to tell him more about her life on Earth. The real stories. The fear and the lies, the scams they'd run and the scrip they'd stolen from anyone they thought could afford it. She wasn't proud of some of her choices, but it was her life and her story, and she wanted him to hear about it someday.

The lesson turned out to be a lot less fun than she'd expected. Instead of a *kes'tarv*, he'd given her a stick. It wasn't as large as hers, and neither end was sharpened. First, he'd show her a move, demonstrating the proper grip and where her feet should be. Then he made her practice it over and over again.

"When do I get to hit something?"

She'd expected him to offer to spar with her. Instead, he led her to the edge of the clearing and pointed to a tree.

"You want me to hit that?"

He nodded.

She whacked it as hard as she could. Her grip was wrong, and the blow stung her hands and made her arms ache. "Ow."

He demonstrated the right grip again and then pointed to the tree.

This time, the strike sounded different and her hands didn't sting. "Oh! I get it now."

That earned her a smile. Striker stepped back, giving her room to go through the entire drill again. By the time she was done, her shoulders ached and her arms felt like they might fall off at any second. But the tree had fresh scars on the bark and the aches she felt were the good kind that meant she'd accomplished something.

"How'd I do?"

"For your first day? Better than I expected. You've fought before." It wasn't a question.

"Where I'm from, if you wanted to keep what you had,

you learned to fight. But street scraps and the occasional bar brawl were part of my old life. I need to prepare for my new one."

"You're already on that path. Come inside. I have something for you."

She fell in behind him and tried not to ogle the fine view she had as they walked around to the front of the cabin. All the cyborgs she'd met were physically perfect, but to her mind, Striker was the best of the bunch.

She wasn't sure if that feeling was mutual, though. Oh, something was definitely going on between them. He didn't like the idea of some other male getting handsy with her. If he wasn't interested in her, he wouldn't care. At least, that was the theory she was going on. If her interest turned out to be one-sided, she was going to need to spend her first paycheck on those ice cream and cookie concoctions Saral and her mates had invented.

The table was set for two, and a plate stacked high with thick-cut sandwiches was set in the middle. "If you're cold, I'll make coffee," he offered.

"All that exercise kept me warm enough, thanks. I could use a drink, though. Water?" she took off her jacket and hung it on a hook by the door. Striker hung his next to it.

"No *ja'kreesh*?" even through the tablet, there was no missing the note of humor in his voice.

"Not this time. That stuff packs a serious punch. If I need it, I'll make myself a small cup at the start of tonight's shift."

"You're working tonight?"

"I am. There's some kind of musical thing going on. One of the colonists puts on a performance night every few weeks. Anya says when they sing the place is always packed."

"I've heard him sing. He's talented."

She tried not to look surprised. "You've been to the Bar None?"

"No. I was at his bonding ceremony, though. He sang Shadow down the aisle. It was nice."

"Wait. The singer is Kade? Shadow's Kade?"

"You didn't know?"

"Everyone here already knows so much about each other I think they sometimes forget that the new arrivals don't have the same information. I've met Kade and Denz, but I didn't make the connection."

"You only feel that way because you haven't met many beings yet. Thousands of colonists live here. Not everyone knows each other."

"The cyborgs do. But I guess that makes sense if you're all from the same place."

"Not all. Shadow was part of a different project."

"She hasn't told us about that yet. She said she would eventually, but we needed to learn other things that were more important than her story."

He snorted. "That's because most of her story is classified."

"Now I really want to hear it. And yours too. Someday. If you want to tell me."

He pointed to the table. "Sit. Eat."

"So, no story?" she asked.

He started making tea and for a few minutes she sat in silence, eating and waiting to see if he answered her.

Eventually, he did. "There isn't much to tell. I was created during the Resource Wars. I fought for two years and watched a lot of good cyborgs die. Afterward, I was part of the rebellion that led to our freedom... only the corporation I worked for didn't free all of us. They incapacitated us with a code word and then shipped us to Reamus Station. When we woke up, our behavioral programming had been augmented, and we were in cages. They tested us. Did experiments. And they made us fight each other and then broadcast the fights for money. I don't know if that was part of the original plan or something our captors came up with later. They'd use the fights to test their modifications. Pitting us against each other."

The moment he started talking about the cages, she'd put down her sandwich. Now her stomach was tied in knots and she had a bitter taste in the back of her mouth that no amount of water could wash away. "I'm so sorry."

"You wanted to hear my story. That's it." He shrugged and turned away from her.

"How many of your own did you have to kill?" she asked softly.

He kept his back turned. "All of them. You're looking at the champion of Reamus Station. I killed them all, Maggie. Including my batch-siblings. That's why Skye warned you about me. I *am* dangerous."

She rose and walked over to him. She could see the tension in his shoulders and neck, like he was carrying the weight of an entire planet. When she got closer, she noted that his hands were fisted in front of him, knuckles white. He was hurting, and she did the only thing she could think of to help. She wrapped her arms around his waist and pressed herself against his back.

"I don't believe that." She'd never believe it. Dangerous men didn't protect strangers without revealing their presence. They didn't share their homes or make tea for guests. As far as she could see, the only person Striker was a danger to was himself.

"You don't know me." He talked to her directly, his voice low and rough.

"I think I do. What happened to you was not your fault. They put you in a horrible place and made you make impossible choices."

A shudder passed through him. "I killed them."

"What would have happened if you hadn't?"

"They would have killed me, and then there would have been no one left to stop their pain."

He tugged her arms away from him and she thought he was pushing her away. He didn't. He turned and wrapped her in his arms instead. There was nothing sexual about his touch. It was simpler than that. He held her tightly and buried his head in her hair, breathing harder now.

"And then what?"

"Then what was left of my friends and family would have had to keep living. They were suffering. In pain. Some of them weren't sane anymore. We all promised each other if that happened…"

"So you kept your promise and helped them escape their suffering." She pressed her head to his chest, the fabric of his shirt soft against her cheek and the steady thump of his heart in her ear.

"I killed them."

"You kept your promise," she repeated.

"You can't understand."

She lifted her head and leaned back so she could see his face. "You're wrong. I do. I left my best friend behind because that's what we agreed to do. She's out there somewhere, alone. Maybe hurt. Maybe dead. And I *left* her. I have to live with that choice, and you have to live with what you've done, but we can't forget that our friends would have done the same thing because that was the deal. And it sucks vacuum."

He was still for a long time and then something seemed to unknot inside him and he let out a slow, drawn breath. "I can't bring back the dead, but maybe… is there a way I can help you find your friend?"

This was it. Her chance to tell him the truth about everything. If she did, though, would he still want to help her? If he knew who she'd been before Haven, would he want to be around her? She didn't want to take that chance. Not yet. "I don't know."

That wasn't a lie. She wasn't sure if he could help. He might be able to access the data locked away inside her arm, but maybe not. And if he did, she had no idea what it was or if it would help them find Jade.

"Alright," his jaw tightened again, and she felt the moment slipping away.

"Thank you for offering. It means a lot to me." She reached up to slip a hand around the back of his neck, drawing his head down as she rose on her toes.

He bowed his head, eyes locked on hers, and she kissed him. It was only going to be a light touch of the lips, but the moment they connected, he uttered a low sound of need that hit her like a comet strike.

The kiss deepened, his hands smoothing up her back to tangle in her hair. He took over, claiming control of the situation with the same confidence he approached everything else.

She allowed it. In fact, she embraced it. Just this once, she didn't want to be the one in control. She wanted to enjoy this moment without worrying about what happened next.

Hard, hungry kisses fueled by need and loneliness were followed by slow, gentle kisses that let her learn the shape of his mouth. He smelled like the forest with a deeper musk that was uniquely his, and his lips tasted of the cookies he'd eaten while he'd watched her train.

She already knew he was strong, but now she took the time to explore his body with her fingers, following the hard lines of muscle and sinew she could feel but not see beneath his shirt.

When her fingers brushed the scar at his throat, he groaned and pulled away. She didn't let him. She took hold of his shirt and held him in place, straining on her toes to reach his mouth again.

"Maggie…" he whispered her name.

"I'm here."

"Why?" There were so many layers of meaning to that question she couldn't count them all.

"Because this is where I'm supposed to be." The words were simple but true.

After that, they stopped talking. There wasn't any need. They communicated by touch, every kiss and caress adding to their silent conversation.

His kisses grew hungry again, demanding more. One hand cupped her breast through her shirt and she wondered what it would feel like when no clothes stood between them.

Her tablet started chiming in insistent tones, dragging her back to reality.

"What is it? An alert? A problem?"

She sighed. "A reminder. I need to get back soon or I won't have time to shower and change before my shift."

"I need to give you something before you leave." Striker's voice came through the tablet speaker this time, and she knew their moment was over. When he let her go, she took a few reluctant steps back, giving him room to move.

"More? I thought lunch was the surprise?"

"Lunch was a necessity. As I understand it, unenhanced humans need to eat regularly, especially if they're exerting themselves."

"Well, that's true. But I brought a couple of food tabs to eat on my way back. I didn't expect you to feed me." She'd have to figure out some other things to bring him. Being indebted to someone wasn't smart and usually ended badly. Even she and Jade had tried to split things fifty-fifty.

"Afraid I'm going to ask you to pay up one day? I won't."

She blushed. Striker knew what she was doing and why. "Sorry. It's not that I don't trust you. It's just that some habits are hard to break."

"I get it. But to borrow a page from Skye's book of favorite phrases, this is Haven. Things are different here." He modulated his voice to sound a little like Skye's.

Maggie burst out laughing. "Does she know you can do that?"

"*Fraxx*, no."

"Can you imitate anyone else?"

His next words came out sounding a lot like her voice. "If I have enough of a vocal sample, I can duplicate almost anyone this way. Only over comms and systems, though."

"Infiltration model." She nodded in understanding. "Handy skill to have."

"It was. Now, it's just a party trick, and I don't do

parties." He reverted to his normal voice. "Finish eating. I'll grab your present."

She sat down and tackled her meal, devouring the rest of her sandwich in quick, hungry bites. She'd need to be going very soon, and she wasn't sure she could trust the tablet to guide her back. "Can you give me a few landmarks to aim for in case this thing craps out again?"

"I'll walk you back myself. I don't want you getting lost."

"Oh! Thank you." More time with Striker was a bonus she hadn't expected. Maybe she'd be able to steal a few more kisses along the way.

"This is for you. If anyone gets *handsy*, use this on them." He set a dagger down on the table beside her. The scabbard was tooled leather dyed a forest-green, and the hilt of the blade was a piece of polished wood stained a deep red. It fit perfectly into her hand, and when she pulled it from the sheath, she stared at the blade in shock.

"It has waves in the metal. It's beautiful!"

"It was hand forged. I don't understand the process, but that is the result. I thought you might like it."

"I do!" She slid it back into its sheath and then got to her feet, moving close enough to hug him. "Thank you. That is the most beautiful thing anyone has ever given me."

"Just remember to use it."

She laughed. "I don't think Anya would appreciate me stabbing the customers. But I will wear it openly and hope they take it as a warning."

"If they touch you, hurt them. They'll learn to behave."

"I need to keep my job, too. Don't worry. I've been doing this a long time, and I know how to handle randy customers. And really, the ones at the Bar None are pretty tame. It's a great place to work." It was safe, clean, friendly, and her pay was three times what she could have earned in her old life. And it wasn't in corporate vouchers, either. It was in hard Vardarian currency she could spend anywhere.

Striker's jaw tightened and he got a stormy look in his eyes.

She laughed and kissed his cheek. "I'll be fine, big guy. Don't worry about me."

She could take care of herself, but she liked that he was worried about her. It was nice to know he cared.

Striker walked her back to the edge of the colony and then waited in the shadows of the trees to make sure she got back to her pod. Once she was inside, he started walking back to his cabin, mulling over the day's events and what he wanted to do next.

He didn't get far before he realized that wasn't the right direction. Tonight, he might need to be somewhere else. First, though, he needed more information. He did something he didn't do often. He called Edge via their internal link.

"What kind of place is the Bar None?" he asked without preamble.

"And hello to you, too. It's a bar. Walls, floor, tables, drinks, and damned good food. Why? Are you actually considering being social for once?"

"No. Maybe. Do they hit on the women there? I heard a lot of flirting goes on."

"You really are spending too much time on your own. Yes, a lot of socializing goes on there, and everywhere else males and

females are together. Your habi-pod was next to mine until we moved to the other side of the river. I know you did your share of socializing. I heard you."

"That was months ago."

"I know." There was a pointed pause. *"So, are you going to the Bar None tonight?"*

"I'm thinking about it."

"It's about time. Do you remember how to do this, or do you need a wingman?"

It took Striker a moment to figure out what Edge meant. He thought Striker was going to find some female company. He didn't bother correcting his friend. *"I can manage on my own, thanks. If you need help though…"*

"No help needed. Enough single Vardarian females are around to keep me busy for years. If you want a drinking partner though, let me know."

"I will. Thanks." He wasn't going to the bar to drink. If he went, it would be to make sure no one bothered Maggie.

He'd tossed the remaining sandwiches into a pack before leaving. He had planned to give them to Maggie, but she'd kissed him goodbye and he'd forgotten about them until she was back inside. She was the only woman he'd ever kissed who could do that to him. When he was with her, he had tunnel vision. All he could see or think about was her.

He fished around in the pack for one of the sandwiches and munched on it as he jogged back to his place.

He should have made sure she ate more before she left. Hell, he hadn't even managed to give her the water she'd asked for. Kissing her had seemed like a much better use of his time. Not that he'd initiated the kiss. He'd been denying his interest in her since the beginning. Because she was human. Because he preferred his own company. And yet somehow, she'd slipped past all his defenses.

"If my batch-siblings could see me now, they'd laugh their asses off." He'd told them so many times to stay alert and never drop their guard. And he'd been blindsided by a redhead with eyes that reminded him of summer in the woods and a laugh as bright as sunlight.

He picked up the pace, and before he'd swallowed the last bite of his sandwich, he'd broken into a run. If Maggie wouldn't protect herself from the patrons of the Bar None, he'd have to do it for her.

8

———

Normally Striker avoided the central bridge that connected the two sides of the colony. It was too crowded and noisy, and he usually ran into at least one being who knew him and wanted to talk.

Tonight was no different. Despite the setting sun and chilly weather, the place was still busy and most of the street vendors were still open and hawking their wares. New carts and stands had appeared since the last time he'd come this way, and some of the originals had expanded their spaces and made them more solid and durable. The colony was maturing. Slowly for now, but he had no doubt the changes to the market area were being repeated all across Haven.

He'd walked past the bar plenty of times but never gone inside. He'd been tempted once or twice by the delicious scents that wafted through the door, but he'd never given in.

The door was closed to keep the cold out, but the moment he pulled it open, warm air redolent with spices and roasted meat washed over him, accompanied by the buzz of voices as the patrons talked and ate.

Several of the cyborgs looked at him in surprise, and a few made a point of looking anywhere but in his direction. Those were the ones who still feared him. After all these months, some still hadn't forgotten who he'd once been. It was another reason he avoided places like this.

"On your left," a familiar voice sounded in his head.

He turned and spotted Ruin seated in a corner with his back to the wall. Wreckage sat across from him, the streaks of white in his dark hair making him easy to recognize even from behind.

He walked over to them and was gratified when Ruin kicked a chair his way.

"Sit."

"Appreciate it." He didn't bother trying to speak aloud.

"Never expected to see you in here. You here for the music, the food, or the booze? The new bartender makes better drinks than the bot. If you're here to drink, be sure to get her to make it," Wreckage said and then nodded toward the bar area.

"And she's easy on the eyes, too," Ruin said.

Maggie was behind the counter, her smile bright as she poured something red into a glass and gave it a quick stir. She looked beautiful. Different. Instead of the battered and worn clothes she usually wore out in the woods, she was dressed in a vivid green top that hugged her curves and was scooped low enough to show an expanse of pale skin and had short sleeves that left her arms bare.

"I'm here to keep an eye on a friend." And judging by the way his friends and many other men present were looking at Maggie, it was a good thing he'd come.

"And here I thought we were your only friends,"

Wreckage said before draining his glass. "It's my turn to talk to the pretty redhead. What are you drinking, Striker? This round is on me."

He was out of his chair in a second, beating Wreckage to his feet. *"I've got this."*

Both men looked surprised but didn't argue. "Afterburners," Ruin said, pointing to their empty glasses. "If you haven't tried it, you should. Tasty and enough of a kick it takes the medi-bots a few minutes to catch up."

Striker nodded and moved toward the bar. He didn't need a drink. He just didn't want Wreckage near Maggie. He trusted the man, but Maggie was busy and didn't need to deal with another flirtatious customer. She had work to do.

The tavern was filling up quickly, and he noted that the stage area was already being set up in preparation for tonight's performance. Servo-droids zipped passed him, delivering food and drink orders to the tables, but a line of customers still waited for Maggie to serve them personally.

All of them were male.

He gritted his teeth. They could use the *vething* droids and save Maggie some work.

He took his place at the end of the line and waited. He could hear everything they said to Maggie. Cyborg and Vardarian alike plied her with jokes, friendly banter, and flattery.

She treated them all the same, with a bright smile and a few cheerful, noncommittal words.

When his turn came, she didn't look up before asking, "And what can I get you tonight?"

"Three Afterburners and an explanation for why you haven't used that dagger yet." He spoke softly, but even still several cyborgs turned to stare when he actually spoke out loud.

She looked up in surprise and then gave a soft squeal of delight. "Striker!"

Her genuine response helped take the edge off his anger. "In the flesh."

"Three Afterburners coming up, and it's nice to see you. Here for the music?"

"No."

"For the food? Got tired of sandwiches?"

"No."

Maggie kept measuring and pouring as she talked. "You came for my soon-to-be-famous cocktails?"

"No."

He pointed to the knife strapped to her hip and then frowned when he saw what she was wearing. Her skirt was jet black and barely covered the tops of her thighs, showing a long expanse of bare legs clad in boots that rose almost to her knees.

His cock came to life instantly as an image of those legs wrapped around his hips popped into his head. "No pants?"

"I get better tips in a skirt," she explained.

He growled.

She laughed. "If you're not here for the food, the booze, or the music, what are you here for?"

"You."

That made her smile. "I'm honored. What table are you at? Once the music starts, I'm going on a break. I could join you if you like?"

"I'd like that." He turned and pointed to his table. "Wreckage and Ruin."

"Oh! That's them? Will you introduce me?"

He managed to swallow back another growl and nodded stiffly. It would be best if she met them here and not in the woods. Plus, he could make it clear that *she* was the one he was here to watch over. "Yes."

"I'll see you later then." Maggie set three drinks down on a tray and pushed it toward him.

There was a credit machine on the tray, too. He ran his hand over it and transferred the scrip for the drinks and a generous tip, too. If she needed money, he'd help. Then she could start wearing pants to work. That skirt looked too good on her. No wonder the customers were flirting.

He carried the drinks back to the table, rearranging his chair so he had a clear view of the bar and Maggie when he sat down.

"So, get anywhere with the redhead?" Wreckage asked.

He took a sip of his drink before answering. It was excellent. *"Her name is Maggie Piper, and she's under my protection."*

Ruin choked on his drink and Wreckage whistled. "How the *fraxx* did you make that happen during a two-minute conversation?"

He explained how he'd met Maggie. The bark spider. The cookies. And the agreement to teach her how to protect herself and navigate the woods.

"But she's human," Ruin pointed out when he was done. "Since when did we start trusting them?"

"I don't trust them. *I trust* her."

They both considered that for a moment and then nodded. There'd been a time they'd looked to him as their leader, and he was gratified to see they still trusted his judgment.

"If you trust her, that's enough for me," Wreckage said.

"Same here," Ruin agreed. "Plus, she's pretty."

"And we do like pretty," Wreckage raised his glass and then grinned at Striker.

"I can hear you grinding your teeth from here. If she's yours, she's yours. No poaching. I owe you too much to do that to you."

Striker snorted. *"She's not mine. She's just under my protection. And if she was? I'm not worried about competition. I'm no prize, but I'm still prettier than either of you."*

Even as he said the words, he wasn't sure how true they were. After the kisses they shared today, she wasn't just someone he wanted to protect anymore. He wanted more. But how much more? He didn't know the answer to that. All he was sure of was he didn't want anyone else taking that choice away from him before he figured it out.

Striker had come to see her.

Maggie couldn't believe it, but all she had to do was look across the room to prove to herself it was real. The man who lived in the woods and rarely spoke to anyone had come into town for her. That was amazing enough, but now she'd seen him all cleaned up... holy *fraxx*. The man was hotter than a supernova. He'd shaved, and she'd been tempted to hop over the bar and kiss him then and there to see if it felt different without the stubble. His outdoor gear had been replaced with a pair of dark slacks and a dress shirt the same shade of blue as his eyes. He could have been a holo-vid actor or one of the celebrity models who sold everything from toothpaste to vacation homes on distant planets.

She kept up her steady flow of light banter with her customers, but every few minutes she would find herself watching Striker again. Every time she looked his way, he was watching her.

"Who is that and why is he looking at you like you're on the menu?" Anya asked a few minutes before the night's entertainment was due to start.

"Who?" Maggie asked, pretending not to know.

"Please. The way you two are making eyes at each other is making me jealous and slightly concerned I'm going to wind up in violation of the decency laws on this planet."

"There are no decency laws on Liberty."

"Good thing, too. So, spill. Who's the hot, broody blond?"

"That's Striker."

"The wild cyborg of the woods? Him? Holy *fraxx*. I was expecting something more like Raze. You know. Beard, long hair. Looks like he's part tree?"

"I've met Raze, yeah. He does look like he's about to start growing leaves." The cyborg Anya described had been the founder of the colony and had spent several years alone on the planet before his now-wife had crash-landed here. It was a romantic story, but once she'd come to Haven and met the couple involved, she'd realized there was a lot more to it than the tale that had reached Earth. There was so much more going on behind the scenes, and she hadn't known any of it. Some she couldn't have known. But some of it she'd deliberately ignored because she'd been too busy trying to survive her own problems to worry about someone else's. Only it turned out, they all had the same problem—the corporations.

"Are there any more like him out there? I might need to take up hiking. You know, for my health." Anya grinned.

"The two he's sitting with spend a fair bit of time out in the woods, too. Or so Striker says. I haven't met them yet."

"Then go meet them now and let me know if they're single. Go on, shoo. You're officially on your break. You find out if they're single, and I'll tell you what I found out when I talked to Phaedra today."

"You talked to her?" Maggie felt a surge of hope. Phaedra was her best chance of tracking down Jade or at least finding some hint as to where she'd gone.

"I did. She's going to help. Details later. Go grab your food and take your break."

"Thank you! She gave Anya's hand a quick squeeze and darted through the door to the kitchen.

Saral waved a spoon in her direction. "Hello. Anya said you'd be coming for your dinner. N'tev's just plating it up."

"Thanks."

"How's the energy out there?" Saral asked.

"Packed house, good buzz, no problems."

"My favorite kind of night," N'tev said, turning to offer her a tray. The pasta dish she'd ordered looked perfect, but two other plates sat on the tray as well. One was a double serving of the new dessert with her cookie recipe, and the other was a platter of fried tubers smothered in dark gravy and topped with chunks of soft, melting cheese.

"I didn't order all that."

"Anya told us to add the dessert and the *pora*. She thought you might want to bring it over to the guy who won't stop staring at you." All three cooks grinned at her. "Who is he?"

"You're all in on this conspiracy?"

"We're old and mated. Let us have this one moment of excitement," Saral said.

"Not that old, my *mahaya*," N'tev rumbled.

"I think our beloved is feeling neglected. Three do you think? Or four?" Antas asked. He was flipping a spatula between his fingers as he eyed his mate with blatant hunger.

"Four," N'tev stated.

Saral shivered, her golden skin taking on a metallic sheen.

"Four?" Maggie asked, too curious to be discreet. Not that the Vardarians would mind. They were far more open about their sexuality than most humans.

"Orgasms," Saral explained with a wicked little smile that flashed her fangs.

"Lucky you."

"My *anrik* and I are the lucky ones," Antas said. "Now, who is the male?"

"His name's Striker. The one from the woods."

"Ah. And he's come to town just to see you?" Saral asked.

"It appears so." She blushed a little, a ribbon of hope and desire unfurling deep inside.

"Then go to him. Feed him. Enjoy," N'tev said.

"And make sure you get at least two orgasms tonight!" Saral called out as Maggie turned to go.

"He's only a friend!"

"Bah. He's here to see you. Orgasms are coming. Enjoy them!"

She could only hope the heavy door had muffled Saral's last words enough no one could have heard. Bracing herself, she walked out of the kitchen and into the front of the house.

Thankfully, the only one laughing was Anya. "They

made you blush? Dammit. Now I owe them an extra night off."

"With pay!" N'tev called out through the still-closing door.

"Yeah, yeah," Anya called back. She didn't look at all concerned about losing. Then she turned and said in a normal tone, "Kade's running behind, so you've got time to talk before the music starts."

"Thank you."

"No, thank you. This night has already been the most successful one yet. They love your drinks and you've got a real way with the customers. I'm glad to have you on the team."

High on Anya's compliments and buzzing with anticipation, Maggie made her way through the throng. She balanced the loaded tray on one hand and kept her other free to swat at anyone who tried to get touchy-feely on her way by. This time, no one tried anything.

Striker got to his feet and took the tray before she reached the table, setting it down at an empty space and a chair he'd found for her. He waited until she was seated before reclaiming his place beside her, demonstrating an unexpected level of manners.

He cleared his throat and then pointed to the man to her left. "Wreckage." He said, his voice its usual roughened growl. Then he pointed to the man beside Wreckage. "Ruin."

He pointed at her this time. "Maggie."

"We met at the bar earlier," Ruin said. "I didn't know you were a friend of Striker's. Sorry if I came on a little strong."

"You didn't. After all, you'll never get a fish to bite if you don't throw out some bait."

"You fish?" Wreckage asked.

"A little," she admitted, setting down her dinner and then placing the *pora* in the middle of the table with utensils enough for everyone.

Ruin leaned forward, curious. "I didn't know Earth still had fish. I thought it was too *fraxxed* up to support life outside the hive cities."

"You're right. No fish in the wild, but most hive cities had tame schools as part of the water purification process. As kids we'd go down to the smaller pools and try to catch the perch. We couldn't eat them because of the biohazard risk, but it was something to do."

"Fish you couldn't eat?" he asked, using his voice again.

"The small ones, no. When they got bigger, they were moved to larger tanks with cleaner water. Once the level of sewage reached safe levels, the fish were harvested and a new batch was cloned."

"Sewage? They swam in that and then you ate them?" Ruin's voice carried the same horror Striker felt.

"Not everyone could afford vat-grown proteins. It was that or eat rats, and I've eaten my share of those, too. Honestly, at least you knew where the fish had been."

She dug into her meal with relish while the men watched her. "Humans are hardier than I thought," Wreckage said. "Is this for us?"

"It is. Sorry. I should have mentioned that. Dig in. All of you." She pointed her fork at the dessert. "Anya sent that along, too. It's made from the same cookie recipe I baked for you. It's amazing."

Striker eyed the savory dish and then the dessert. She knew which one he was going to go for before he picked up his fork—the dessert.

One bite later he made a low sound of pleasure that rolled through her like the buzz of her favorite sex toy—which had been getting a lot of use in the last few days.

"Good, isn't it? I tried to get them to call it 'Better than Sex,' but Anya vetoed it." She realized her mistake the second the words left her mouth.

Striker's eyes darkened and the other two grabbed spoons and stole bites of the dish while he was distracted.

"Mine. Get your own," Striker snarled at them and then took another spoonful and held it out to her. "Taste."

"I know what it tastes like…"

"Now."

Fraxx, it wasn't fair how sexy he was when he got this growly. She did what she was told, and he fed her the dessert. It really was delicious. She decided to get a little payback and licked the spoon as he withdrew it, moaning softly as she did.

"*That* is good. Sex with me would be better," he said.

She nearly combusted right there in her seat and the part of her brain that controlled speech short-circuited.

Ruin barked out a sharp laugh and leaned back in his chair. "I'm going to take your word on that."

"And I'm going to order us our own bowl of bliss. What is this stuff called, Maggie?"

It took her far too long to form her next words. "It's on the menu as 'Almost Heaven,' and it's tonight's special." Then she looked at Striker and smiled, hoping like hell she wasn't about to put her foot in her mouth. "Unlike these two, I'm interested in doing a direct comparison anytime you are."

Before either of them could say anything else, the lights dimmed and a moment later the small stage was illuminated by a spotlight drone hovering overhead. A tall, gold-skinned Vardarian walked into the light carrying something similar to a guitar. Kade walked with confidence and settled himself in the spotlight with all the poise of a professional entertainer. He strummed the instrument several times, making small adjustments.

From somewhere in the darkness, a woman's voice called out. "You already tuned your *saryk* at home, my *mahoyen*. We want to hear you sing!"

There was a ripple of laughter from the crowd at Shadow's teasing words.

"Hush, my *dyna*. I'm getting there," Kade replied, turning to look in the direction of his mate.

Maggie didn't need to see her to know who he was looking at. His adoring expression made it very clear. While Kade finished warming up, she took a few more bites of her dinner and then turned her chair around so she could watch the performance while still being able to reach her food. Her break would end before the concert did, and she wouldn't get a chance to eat again until her shift ended.

The new position meant she was closer to Striker. So close their legs were touching. It was like they were connected by an invisible power cord and even the smallest movement generated a fresh wave of sparks.

Kade was good. The song was in Vardarian, but it didn't matter. The music carried her away despite the fact she could only understand a few words. As the first song ended, Striker reached back and retrieved their dessert. He moved it between them, balancing the bowl in one large hand with his knuckles resting on her thigh as he offered her a spoon.

She flashed him a smile. "Thank you."

The next two songs were just as entertaining. At least,

she thought they were. It was hard to be sure if the music or the moment made her feel so happy. Here she was on a new planet, at her new job, surrounded by kind beings and sharing chocolate with a sexy cyborg who made her heart race and starred in every erotic fantasy she'd had since the day they'd met. This was the best day of her life. The only thing that would have made it better is if Jade were here, too.

They finished the dessert as the next song ended, and Kade announced he'd be taking a pause before coming back for another set. Her comm buzzed in her pocket, announcing that her break was about to end.

"I need to get back to work," she murmured.

"I'm staying to walk you home," Striker informed her.

She pretended he'd given her a choice. "I'd like that. It's sweet of you to offer."

She gathered up their empty plates and stacked them back on the tray. "I'll send some fresh drinks over, too. Wreckage and Ruin, a pleasure to meet you both."

"Same."

"Yeah."

The lights were still dimmed, but she'd spent years working in semi-darkness. She lifted the tray and then bent down to brush a quick kiss to Striker's cheek. "I'll see you later."

"Yes, you will." And damned if his low, gravelly voice didn't have her blushing as she walked away, adding an extra sway to her hips as she went. She was so distracted with thoughts of Striker she forgot to be on guard for wandering hands, and the pinch to her ass was hard enough to make her yelp in surprise.

Before she could do more than swat at the offender's

hand, she heard an enraged bellow and something large, heavy, and very pissed came thundering up behind her.

Being in the middle of a bar fight was never a good thing, but she'd been here before and knew what to do. She dropped the tray onto the nearest table and then dove underneath it, scrambling past customers' legs and out the other side.

By the time she was back on her feet, the fight was over.

Striker had another cyborg down on his knees, head bowed, body painfully arched to try to take some of the pressure off the arm Striker held in one vicious grip. He was snarling at the other cyborg, teeth bared and his face a mask of fury. "She's mine."

"Sorry, Striker. I... I didn't know."

"Doesn't matter. You don't touch what isn't yours. You know this. We're not humans. We're better than them!"

"Yes."

Now she could see why Skye had warned her about Striker. Skye had seen this side of him back on Reamus. Of course she'd be worried.

Maggie wasn't.

"Let him go, Striker. You made your point."

His head snapped up. "Did he hurt you?"

"No. He surprised me. Now, let him go. You can't start roughing up the other customers just because you don't like what they're doing."

"He touched you!"

She walked around the table and set her hand on his arm. "And I was handling it. That's part of the job."

"I don't like your job."

"Tough. I do. You don't own me, Striker. One make-out

session doesn't even give you the right to comment on my shoes, never mind interfere with my job."

His gaze dropped to her legs. "I like the boots. Your skirt is too short."

The lights all came on, leaving everyone blinking. When her vision returned, Anya was standing nearby with a pulse rifle in her hands. "Maggie, are you okay? Do we have a problem?"

"I'm fine. It's fine. One of these fellows pinched my ass and the other has a bad case of over-protective-itis."

"Thrash, is that true? Did you pinch Maggie?"

"Yeah." Thrash said, looking sheepish.

Anya sighed. "You going to do it again?"

"*Fraxx*, no."

"Good. Then I don't need to shoot you." She raised her voice to a shout that carried across the tavern. "No one touches my staff. You want to fight each other, fine. But take it outside. If you don't, I will shoot you. Striker, you can let him go now."

Striker nodded and released the man's arm.

"Thank you." Anya looked at him thoughtfully. "You want to make sure no one bothers Maggie again?"

Striker nodded.

"Great. You're on the payroll. Your job is to make sure everyone remembers their manners. Sound good?"

"Yes."

Maggie stormed over to Striker. "Oh hell no. This is not happening. You're going to say no."

He shook his head.

"Anya? You're really going to do this?"

The older woman shrugged. "Sorry, hon. I've needed a bouncer longer than I've needed a bartender. Your man said all the right things, and he controlled the situation without doing any damage."

Her man? Seeing she wasn't going to get any help from that quarter, Maggie turned back to Striker. "You can't stroll in and take over my life."

"I'm not taking over. I'm protecting you."

"That's not your job."

"It is. I'm your protector."

"Since when?" she demanded.

"Since before we met. I have always protected you, Maggie."

His words filled her stomach with giant, mutant butterflies. It was true. He'd kept her safe in the woods. Saved her life, probably more than once.

"I think I liked it better when you didn't talk so much," she muttered.

He grinned and held out his hand.

She was tempted to ignore it, but that wasn't what she wanted to do. Not really. She slipped her hand into his, and he pulled her into his arms, kissing her hard on the mouth before picking her up and putting her over his shoulder.

"I will be back tomorrow to discuss hours and pay. Maggie and I are taking the rest of the night off. You can pay her out of my wages for the lost hours."

"What? No! Put me down! Dammit, Striker. I have to get back to work."

He slapped a hand on her ass hard enough to sting. "Stop squirming."

"Jerk!"

"Mags?" Anya asked, the single word loaded with meaning. If Maggie didn't want this, all she had to do was say so, and Anya would take care of it.

Maggie raised her head, which wasn't easy in her current position, and managed to catch Anya's eye. "I'm fine. *He* might not be. I'm really sorry about this."

Her boss relaxed but then nodded. "Don't be." She paused and then smirked before adding. "Just remember what Saral said. Make sure you get at least two!"

Maggie blushed and dropped her head without saying another word. She had no idea where they were going or what was going to happen next, but she couldn't help but hope her friends were right and orgasms were coming her way… soon.

9

THIS NIGHT HAD NOT GONE the way he'd expected. He'd come because someone needed to watch out for Maggie and she didn't have anyone else. Now, he had a job he hadn't been looking for and every intention of taking her back to his place to prove once and for all that he was better than any dessert in existence.

It was time to accept reality. This had never been about protecting Maggie for the sake of the colony, or herself. He'd done it because he wanted to. Because he wanted *her*. A human. It was hard to believe, but it was happening.

"Are you going to put me down anytime soon? I don't know where the hell we're going, and I'm not really enjoying being upside-down after eating all that food."

"My place." His throat was raw from all the talking he'd done, so he deactivated his pain receptors. He needed to be able to communicate.

He waited for her response, not sure if she'd protest. If she did, he'd respect her choice. He really hoped she didn't.

"Okay. But if we're going to be traipsing through the

woods, I'm going to need to change first. Plus, my jacket is still at the bar."

Her jacket. *Fraxx.*

His medi-bots helped regulate his body temperature, so he'd forgotten how cold it was outside. With no coat and that short skirt…

He set her down gently and then unbuttoned his shirt.

"What are you doing?"

"You're cold. I'm not." He stripped off the shirt and wrapped it around her shoulders. It was so large on her that it covered more of her legs than the skirt did. Now he was the only one who could see her legs, he regretted the need to hide them, but it would take a few minutes to reach his home and she needed to stay warm.

He expected her to button up, but instead she walked up to him and placed both hands on his bare chest.

Her fingers were cool, but her touch was like flames on his skin. "You are… wow."

"So are you." He covered one of her hands with his and wrapped the other around her back, pulling her in snugly against him. She raised her head and uttered a soft gasp as their bodies met. He leaned down and kissed her, claiming her mouth with his and letting the taste of her brand itself on his senses.

When she moaned, he felt it as much as heard it, a buzz against his lips and tongue that was sweeter than any music.

Hunger tore through him, awakening base needs he'd tried to bury and ignore. Every cell in his body burned with desire for the woman in his arms. "Will you come home with me?" His voice was so raw and rough with need he wasn't sure she'd understand him. He swallowed hard and was about to try again when she rose up on her toes and pressed a finger to his lips.

"Yes. I'll go home with you."

He scooped her into his arms and set off at a jog toward the artists' quarter. His home was there, on the outermost edge of the colony.

"Um. I know I got lost already today, but isn't your home in the other direction?" She pointed back toward the bridge.

"Cabin that way. Home this way."

She shivered, and he broke into a run. He had to get her inside before she got any colder.

"You have a home in *town*?"

"Yes." Everyone did. It was how Haven worked. Every citizen had all they needed to live. Housing, food, and the basic comforts of life were available to every citizen.

She poked him in the shoulder with surprising force. "You jerk! I thought you lived in the woods."

"I do. Sometimes."

"Sometimes. But the rest of the time you have running water, electricity, and I bet you even have a food dispenser."

"Yes."

"And I made you cookies!" there was no missing the upset in her tone.

He reached the gate to his small front yard and popped it open with one hip. "Why are you unhappy?"

"Because I thought I was giving you something special. Something you couldn't make for yourself at the touch of a button."

"You did."

"How?" her face was pressed into his shoulder now, hiding her expression.

He didn't answer right away. He wanted to get inside before he explained. He reached out and connected to his home's systems, switching on the lights and opening the door as he came up the walk.

Once they were inside with the door closed, he set her gently down in front of him. "Look at me."

She raised her head, his heart twisting when he saw her tear-filled eyes.

He was tempted to speak to her through his home's speakers, but this was too important. "No one has ever given me a gift before. Not once. And you made those cookies yourself. With your own hands. It was..." He touched a finger to her cheek. "I will never forget my first gift."

"Oh." She exhaled softly and then turned her head to nuzzle his hand. "Good. That's good. Not that you've never had a gift before, but that it was special. I wanted it to be." Maggie took his hand in hers and then took a look around.

"If this is where you live, why is there more furniture in your cabin?" She gestured to the mostly empty rooms with her free hand, a look of stunned bewilderment on her face.

"I have all I need." And he did. A table with two chairs. A deep pile of cushions mounded up on the floor and covered in a handwoven blanket he'd picked up from a weaver who lived just down the way. It had all the colors of the forest in it—greens and browns with hints of gold here and there. He could watch holo-vids and other broadcasts from there if he was so inclined.

Dishes were stacked in the cupboards with linens and towels in the closet. Not to mention a separate bedroom housed a bed so large he could stretch out comfortably for the first time in his life. Even his showers were indulgent. Plenty of hot water, and he'd bought some handmade soaps and shampoo from another neighbor. He liked the way they smelled, like spring mornings and the forest after it rained.

As far as he was concerned, he lived in a palace with more space than he needed and comforts he couldn't have imagined during his years of captivity.

"Maybe." Maggie's fingers tightened around his. "But it's not all you deserve. You're free now. You can have more than this."

He chuckled at the irony of her words. She had less than this and had spent weeks scavenging for used and imperfect items she could stash away in case she needed them when she could have simply requisitioned new ones.

"Right now, I have everything I want." He pulled her into his arms and kissed her again. She'd pulled her hair back in a ponytail, which made it easy to wrap the strands around his hand. When he tugged her head back, she moaned and her eyes fluttered closed. He could sense her arousal, the way her pulse raced and her body temperature rose as he took control.

He hummed in approval and set his hand, still holding hers, on her waist. His need was a physical ache now, an all-consuming fire that had been left untended for too long. He glanced down the hall to his room.

Too far away.

His gaze landed on the mound of cushions in the living room. Perfect.

She moved in a slow, sinuous dance, grinding their bodies together as his tongue tangled with hers.

He walked them both backward, guiding her with his hands and body. She moved willingly, responding to his touch with absolute trust, her eyes still closed as her breath mingled with his.

Fire streaked through him. She'd surrendered to him, trusted him to take care of her. At one time he'd been certain he'd never want that responsibility again. He'd been wrong. If that was the price for having Maggie in his arms, he'd pay it—at least for tonight.

When they reached the pile of pillows, he stopped walking and started to strip her out of her clothes. He wanted to tear them off of her, but he knew she wouldn't appreciate it. Like him, she valued what little she had.

She started undressing him, too, undoing the belt at his waist and dropping it at their feet. It would have been faster if they'd focused on themselves instead of each other, but he couldn't keep his hands off of her. He reclaimed his shirt and then removed hers. The more skin he revealed, the harder he got until his cock was throbbing in time to his heartbeat. She undid his pants and slipped her fingers around his thick shaft, tearing a groan from his chest as she cooed in delight.

"So, the rumors are true…" she murmured.

"Only rumors, though?" The thought that she'd done this with another cyborg crashed through his head like an enraged beast.

She tightened her grip on him and looked up, hazel eyes bright with need. "You're the first man I've been with in a long time, Striker."

"Good."

A flash of wariness darkened her eyes and she let go of him, leaning back. "And you? How many females have you been with since you came here? Is that something else you haven't told me? Like this house? Do you have a girlfriend?"

He curled his lip back in a snarl. "No girlfriend. No females. Not for months. I was happy alone."

"Good," she threw his one-word response back at him.

Her skirt hit the ground, and he forgot to breathe. She was wearing a tiny scrap of black lace that barely covered her pussy. She might as well have been naked under her skirt. *Veth.* If he'd known…

"You like?" She flashed him a brazen grin and bent down to release the fitting on her boots. "I was wearing those during our training session today, too."

He expelled a sharp breath and tried to find something to say. He couldn't. "That… I…" he stammered, his brain failing to form a complete thought.

"Speechless? And you've been so chatty tonight."

He tore off his pants the rest of the way, kicking off his shoes hard enough one of them hit the far wall.

She yelped, laughed, and took two steps back from him. "Ooh, is this when you go all big bad cyborg on me?"

He didn't say a word. He just nodded once and closed the distance between them so fast she didn't have time to move. Not that she tried. She wanted this as much as he did, and knowing that unlocked something inside of him.

If she wanted to play… he could, too.

Maggie knew she was pressing Striker's buttons. She knew, but she couldn't stop herself. She wanted to see who he was under the growliness he wore like body armor. She wanted to break through and reach the man buried beneath the scars and guilt.

When he came after her, she was ready. Her arms ached from fight practice, but she caught hold of his shoulders as he swept her off her feet and carried her down onto the bed of pillows.

She clung to him, laughing as they tumbled into the soft nest. Somehow he managed to roll them so he landed first, cushioning her against his big body.

His mouth found hers, arms like steel bands wrapping around her as he flipped them again, pinning her beneath him.

"No more talking." He placed one hand beside her shoulder and pushed up in a display of strength that made her head spin and her blood sing.

"You mean you're not talking anymore? Or are you telling me I can't talk anymore? Because that's really not going to work for me." She licked her lips and grinned.

He didn't answer her aloud, but his mouth quirked up into a smile that sent thrills chasing down her spine. He shifted, pressing a knee between her legs until she spread them enough for him to move between her thighs.

"I'm still not clear on the rules. Am I allowed to talk or —oh!" she broke off as Striker pressed a callused thumb to her clit, rubbing it in small, tight circles.

The sexy little smirk on his face told her he knew exactly what he was doing to her and was enjoying every second of it.

So was she.

"So… no talking?" She managed to get the words out in a soft, breathy gasp as she rocked her hips against his fingers.

This time, he slid a thick finger into her channel and started fucking her with it, his thumb still working her clit at the same time.

"You're still not answer—" she lost the ability to form words as he added another finger.

He was kneeling between her legs, out of her reach, so she had to settle for gripping the blanket beneath her as he worked her body like a maestro playing his favorite instrument. Time blurred and her focus narrowed until nothing remained in their universe but the two of them and the pleasure coursing through her.

Her orgasm came on with breath-stealing speed, her cries ringing off the walls of the near-empty room as she bucked and arched against his hand.

She collapsed back onto the pillows, limbs boneless, her whole body buzzing with the aftershocks. It took most of her will just to lift her head to watch as Striker withdrew his hand and raised it to his lips, sucking her cream from his fingers with the same intensity as he'd consumed the dessert they'd shared.

He grabbed several of the pillows and rearranged them before shifting positions so he was sitting down, legs outstretched, the hard ridges of his abdomen flexed and perfect as he pointed to her and then crooked his finger.

This time, she decided to keep her mouth shut. Without a word she rose and crawled over to him, her movements as slow and sensual as she could manage. It didn't matter that she'd just had a mind-blowing orgasm, her body wanted more.

The moment she was within reach he reached up and undid the tie holding back her hair, wrapping it around his fingers and using it to pull her in for another kiss.

His free hand took one of hers, guiding and balancing her as she straddled his heavy thighs and pressed her wet pussy along the shaft of his cock.

They both groaned, their kiss becoming more urgent as she rocked her hips, every move increasing the friction between them. He tore his mouth from hers, tugging on her hair until she tipped her head to one side and bared her throat. He kissed his way down to her collarbone, nipping and nuzzling at her tender skin. She'd have marks there in the morning, but right now she didn't care. That was a problem for her future self to deal with.

Striker kept working his way lower until his lips found her nipple and he sucked it into the heat of his mouth. She gasped and then squirmed as his teeth closed over the pebbled nipple with the perfect amount of force. He was pushing without hurting her, learning her boundaries and claiming her body one kiss at a time.

She wrapped a hand around his neck, holding him to her as she bowed her head to blow gently in his ear.

He shuddered, his cock twitching against her folds. "Like that?" her voice was barely more than a whisper, fanning more of her breath across his ear.

He growled something incoherent, a sound, not a word. Laughing, she ran the tip of her tongue along the curve of his ear and then down to the lobe to draw it into her mouth.

This time the sound he made was half-wild, the vibration of it rolling through her. He bucked his hips hard, lifting them both off the floor as his cock slid over her clit again.

It was exquisite, intense, and not nearly enough. "More."

Fingers tightened in her hair, their heads rising at the same time. His mouth crashed against hers, hungry and demanding.

Callused hands slipped to her shoulders and then down to her hips, leaving trails of fire in their wake. He gripped her hips and lifted her off him, their kiss breaking for a moment as he positioned her and then brought her down on the thick head of his cock.

He held her like that for several seconds. She dangled in the air with only the backs of her feet touching the floor, her entire body throbbing with the need to have him inside her.

She cupped his face in her hands, looking into his eyes, and saw desire there. Raw and primal. But something else was there, too, something she hadn't expected —vulnerability.

She whispered his name and then leaned in to kiss him. As their mouths met, he lowered her into his lap, easing himself into her passage as he did. Gazes locked, bodies pressed together, the intensity between them built as he filled her.

Neither of them moved for several seconds, but then impatience drove her to action. She flexed her inner walls around him and rocked her hips, pushing him just a little deeper.

Striker groaned, arching into her, and the next thing she knew the world spun and she was on her back again, pressed down into the pillows as Striker took control.

"That didn't take long," was all she managed to say before his mouth was on hers and he was moving over her, driving his hard length into her body with long, powerful thrusts.

His kisses were bruising, his touch demanding as every stroke unleashed a fresh wave of ecstasy. Maggie moaned into his mouth, her nails digging into the curve of his shoulders as she clung to him and met his every movement with one of her own.

She wrapped one leg around his thigh, using the leverage it created to take him deeper. Within seconds his hand wrapped around the back of her knee, drawing her leg higher and holding her there. She was pinned beneath him now, wide open and unable to do anything but accept the pleasure he offered.

The end came too quickly for her, the constant barrage of pure pleasure tipping her over into a breathless orgasm that tore through her with all the fury of a storm.

As she arched and shuddered beneath him, Striker's rhythm faltered, his strokes coming faster, her name a near silent whisper on his lips.

"Yes. Oh yes!" she called out. She needed to see him lose control. To feel him empty himself inside her.

His cock twitched, his pace accelerating. He broke their kiss to raise his head and roar as he reached his climax, his wordless cry ringing out as he drove himself into her one last time. Then, he slumped over her, keeping most of his weight on his hands as he buried his head in the crook of her shoulder.

She held him, stroking his hair and making soft noises of contentment she hadn't known she was capable of making.

When he finally raised his head, his expression was softer than she'd ever seen it. "Beautiful," he said and then brushed a tender kiss to her lips.

"So, now we're talking again?" she quipped, deflecting the compliment.

"I am. You were already warned what happens when you speak." He winked and kissed her again before easing himself out of her body and flopping onto the floor beside her.

"I'm pretty sure I'm safe for a little while. I mean, not even cyborgs can recover that fast. Right?"

His answer was a grin so wicked it would have done

the devil proud. He took her hand and guided it down to his cock. It was already hard again. "Wrong."

"Oh *fraxx*," she murmured, wrapping her fingers around him.

"And yet, you're still talking."

She leaned in and kissed him. "So are you."

He growled, speared his hands into her hair, and kissed her so hard she saw stars. If this was how she was destined to die, she was totally at peace with it. Being with Striker would be worth it.

10

<hr>

"You're spending more time in town these days," Edge commented as they ran through the silent streets of Haven.

Striker liked the colony when it was like this—quiet and still, with most of the inhabitants still sleeping. "*The rockclaws are starting to hibernate and I'm waiting on some materials for the cabin,*" he sent via their internal channel.

Edge shot him a look that made it clear he wasn't buying it. "Materials, huh? You sure it isn't because of the human you carried out of the Bar None the other night? I hear you even have a job now. You. Working. In town. For a human."

"*You've been trying to get me to pick a profession since we got here.*"

"True. Working as bar security wasn't what I thought you'd pick, but if you're happy..." Edge's words packed enough subtext to fill a cargo deck.

"*You have something to say about my recent decisions?*" They flew past their friend Denz for the second time that morning. He waved as they passed him. Denz wasn't a cyborg and couldn't keep up with them, but they still ran "together" a few days a week. Most of the cyborgs thought they were crazy, but Striker liked it. Until the last few days, running, sparring, and his time in the woods were the only ways he had to burn off excess energy. Now... now he had Maggie, too.

"It's your human. Skye's a little worried about her."

Striker sped up as a surge of resentment hit him. First Skye warned Maggie to stay away from him, now this. *"Skye needs to worry about the human females still trying to acclimatize to life here. Maggie isn't her responsibility anymore."*

Edge caught up within a few seconds and matched Striker's new pace. "You know why that isn't easy for her."

"I do. That doesn't change the facts. Maggie doesn't need Skye's protection. She has mine."

Edge did a double take and nearly tripped over his own feet. "Say that again."

"I don't need to. You have perfect recall of every conversation we've ever had."

They ran the last hundred meters to their usual stopping point, a bare patch of ground just outside the *gharshtu* pens.

"Yeah, but I'm saving that for later when I'm trying to convince myself I didn't imagine this whole conversation. When did you start trusting *them*?"

"I don't. I trust Maggie." He paused and then added, *"And Denz, Sevda, and Phaedra. I'm coming to like Anya, too. She asked about you, by the way. I gather you haven't been around for your weekly chat about Zero-G hockey. She wanted to know if you were okay."*

Edge looked sheepish for a second and then laughed.

"Okay, I like *some* humans. Not all of them are a waste of atmosphere."

"*Some*," Striker agreed. He wasn't giving the whole human race a pass because Maggie and the small cohort of humans in Haven hadn't tried to enslave anyone or destroy this world the way they had Earth.

"So. This thing with the human…"

Striker answered him with a swat to the arm. "*Her name is Maggie. And when did you get this nosey?*"

"Maggie. Right. This thing with Maggie. It's serious?"

He shrugged. "*It's* something." Being with her made him happy. She was a bright light in the gray twilight of his existence. He wasn't ready to put any of that into words, though. Not yet. They *were*. That was enough for him.

Denz caught up to them, his arrival stirring up the *gharshtu*. The flightless birds were big, vile tempered, and dangerous. They were also tasty and fierce enough to fight back against most of the local predators and win, which was why they were so common in Vardarian colonies.

"You two look serious. You telling him about the platforms?"

Edge shook his head.

Striker shrugged. "He's being nosy. Wants to know about Maggie."

Denz looked momentarily startled, and Striker realized he'd been speaking aloud.

"Yeah. He talks now," Edge said. "This woman must be magical."

Striker jabbed two fingers into the air in an obscene gesture, and both men laughed.

"I heard. You and the new bartender. This keeps up and Anya is going to need to post a sign warning patrons that drinking at the Bar None can lead to relationships." Denz pointed to himself and then Striker. "You. Me. And I heard a pair of Vardarians found their *mahaya* there last week."

Edge nodded. "Talia."

Talia was like River and Skye. She'd been created after the war with behavior mods that made her more nurturing and almost shy in comparison to most of her brethren. Striker had heard the rumors, of course, but he'd been too distracted by his own situation to pay much attention.

"She's happy?" Denz asked.

"Overjoyed," Edge said, his voice dryer than dust.

"Relax, I'm *fairly* sure it's not contagious."

Edge snorted. "Think I'll stay away from the Bar None for a while, anyway. Just in case."

"It's not so bad. Is it, Striker?" Denz asked and grinned at him.

He smiled back and flashed a thumbs up. Not only in agreement, but because he was enjoying teasing Edge. The surly cyborg was even more solitary than he was, at least when it came to female company.

After a moment, he pointed upward and then raised his brows in query.

"Yeah, the platforms. There's a problem," Denz said, his tone darkening.

"A big one," Edge agreed. "But you're going to be one of the first to know, so… discretion is needed."

He touched a finger to his lips and then made a locking gesture.

"The defense grid is down," Denz said grimly.

"When? How?" Striker asked.

"It started acting up a few days ago. Minor outages and glitches at first, but it's turned into a cascade failure.

We've got crews working on a fix here and in orbit, but so far no one's been able to find the problem."

He had no doubt Phaedra would be part of the team dealing with this crisis, and if one of the most talented cyber-jockeys in the galaxy couldn't find the reason for the failure, it wouldn't be an easy fix.

A thought occurred. "Positioning data?"

"Yeah. That's where it started. Yours went out, too?" Edge asked.

"Maggie's." And if that was going to be a concern, he'd have to tell her she couldn't leave the colony. Not until he had some other way of finding her if she got lost again.

"We're vulnerable until that grid is back up. All of us. The prince has every ship we have to spare in orbit, acting as a makeshift blockade, but freighters and shuttles aren't well-armed. They can be used as spotters, but that's about it," Denz said.

"We're going to issue a population-wide warning soon. I wasn't going to mention it until then," Edge glanced at Denz, who shrugged.

"An hour isn't going to make any difference. Striker and Maggie spend a lot of time in the woods. Shadow and I figured he'd want to know that wasn't a good idea for the next while."

He nodded in appreciation. The plan had been for Maggie to come with him today to check the rockclaw traps. That wouldn't happen now, but he knew how to make it up to her. He'd picked up her *kes'tarv* yesterday. He'd give it to her and show her how to use it. He liked that idea. Training led to long, hot showers and even hotter sex.

Maggie might be unenhanced, but she made up for it with passion and an enthusiasm for life that was infectious. She had more energy than should have been possible for someone without nanotech. Once she got her injection… The thought had his cock hardening and he had to refocus on the problem at hand.

The colony was vulnerable. Play time was over… for now.

"Who?" he asked aloud.

"We don't know. It might just be a coding glitch," Denz said.

Striker snorted. The system had worked perfectly for months. The chances that it would suddenly develop an issue on its own were low.

"Yeah. None of us believe that, either. Someone brought it down deliberately."

"Here?" Striker pointed to the ground. If the enemy was on Liberty, they should be hunted down and killed.

"If they're on the planet, they avoided being seen. Bad news is, that probably means they're cloaked. Good news is, if a bunch of ships had tried that, we'd have seen an energy surge. So, it's likely only one or two smaller ships," Edge said.

"Odds are it's miners coming to grab what they can of the tantalum, but in case it's something else we need to be ready for trouble," Denz added.

Striker snarled and tapped the grip of his blaster. Like most of his cyborg brethren, he never left home unarmed. It was part of their conditioning and their commitment to never be taken prisoner again. This was his home, and he'd die defending it. Anyone who threatened this place or its citizens would pay the ultimate price. They should be tracking the intruders down and putting an end to this. Now.

Edge put a hand on his arm. "I know. I want to go after

them, too. But the council isn't ready to take that step." He glared at Denz. "I was outvoted."

"The prince's advisor was right. If we react with violence, the rest of the galaxy is going to take it as proof that they were right about you and the other cyborgs. That you're too dangerous to be allowed off-world. We need more information before we escalate."

"Yardan isn't just an advisor. He's Tyran's *fraxxing* spymaster," Edge spat out the last word with disdain. "If he had his way, we'd just collect information forever and never do a damned thing with it."

"I'm not a soldier, but I know that to win battles, you need good intel," Denz pointed out.

"Intel needs to be shared to be useful. That Vardarian guards it like a *gharshtu* protecting its nest." Edge nodded toward the scaley, three-meter-tall carnivores on the other side of the fence.

"He's as much a member of this community as we are. I trust him," Denz said firmly.

"Does Shadow agree with your assessment?" Edge shot back.

"She does. And you need to stop thinking like that. My *mahaya* may be a cyborg, but she's a citizen of Haven, just like everyone else. There are no sides, here, Edge."

"So you keep saying."

This was an old argument that wasn't going to be resolved any time soon. Striker stopped listening. He had more important things to think about—like Maggie's safety.

"*Things to do. Keep me informed,*" he sent to Edge. Then he waved to Denz and took off at a flat run. Maggie needed to know what had happened and why she wasn't going anywhere near the woods for the next few days.

Maggie heard Striker get dressed to go running, but apart from a vague wave and a mumbled goodbye, she hadn't stirred an inch from her warm cocoon of blankets. She needed more sleep if she was going to keep up to her lover's near insatiable appetites, at least until she'd been on Liberty long enough to qualify for her nanotech injection. Good food and a safe place to sleep had already done wonders to improve her health and fitness. It was hard to imagine feeling any better than she did right now.

The main source of her happiness wasn't the riches of this place, though. It was Striker. He had a playful side she'd never imagined, and the last few days had been filled with more laughter than any other time she could remember. She was truly happy, and that knowledge fed a growing sense of guilt and worry. Jade was still missing, and so far no one had been able to find the slightest trace of her in the real or digital world. The two of them had done this before, disappearing and then reconnecting once it was safe, but it had never taken this long.

Then there was Maggie's other fear. Things with Striker were too good. In her experience, every moment of joy came with an equal amount of pain, and she worried that the bill would come due soon.

"Don't borrow trouble," she muttered to herself as she grudgingly got out of bed. There was no point in trying to get back to sleep once her mind started churning. She might as well find some caffeine and get an early start to the day.

The door chimed before she even made it to the kitchen.

"Morning people are the worst. Doesn't anyone sleep

in around here?" Maggie looked down at herself and sighed. She was wearing one of Striker's shirts, mismatched socks, and her hair was an uncombed mess. But given it wasn't dawn yet, whoever was at the door could deal with her appearance or come back later. *Much* later.

"Who is it and why are you awake?" she asked as she approached the door.

"It's Skye."

"Did you bring coffee?"

She heard a soft laugh on the other side of the door. "No. But I needed to see you." There was a hushed urgency to Skye's words that made the hair on the back of Maggie's neck rise.

She opened the door with a touch of her hand and was nearly trampled by Skye as she rushed inside. Shadow followed at a more sedate pace, looking slightly bemused.

"You're okay!" Skye grabbed Maggie in a hug so fierce her ribs creaked.

"I am. Or I will be once I have a hot coffee in my hand. What the *fraxx* is going on?"

"Skye was worried about you," Shadow said, looking around the almost-empty room. "Not much for décor. Is he?"

"It's a work in progress." Maggie untangled herself from Skye. "Why are you worried?"

"Striker beat up someone and then *carried* you out of the Bar None, and you haven't come to classes since," Skye said.

So that was it. "Caffeine. I am not having this conversation until I have caffeine."

"And maybe some pants," Shadow suggested. "You dress. I'm on coffee duty."

"Pants are not required before sunrise, but if you're making me coffee? I'll make an exception this one time."

She kept Striker's shirt on but added a pair of pants and ran a comb through her hair before rejoining the others. Shadow handed her a mug and then looked at the two chairs. "I guess we're doing this standing."

"Sorry. Striker isn't one for having visitors over. You two sit, I'll stand."

Once they were settled, Maggie started talking. "I know I haven't been to my classes, but I did send messages telling you I'd be back next week. Things are…" she waved a hand. "In flux."

"But you're okay? You're not hurt?"

"Striker wouldn't hurt me. If you thought he might, you would have said something before now. I've just been busy. I've got shifts at the bar, and Striker's been training me to protect myself, which involves a lot of hitting things with a stick."

"But he took you…" Skye groaned and closed her eyes. "I thought I might have been wrong about him."

"Which is why you showed up now, when he's out running with his friends." Maggie looked at Shadow. "Including one of your mates. Does Denz know you're here?"

"No. But Kade does. I'm just here in case Skye was right. I'm glad she wasn't. I like Striker."

"So do I." Maggie turned to her friend. "Skye, Striker didn't beat up anyone. Thrash groped me. Striker reacted badly. No one got hurt. He carried me off, but once we were outside, he asked my permission to take me to his place, and he even gave me his shirt so I wouldn't get cold on the way."

Skye exhaled. "Okay. Good. I just… You don't know what he's capable of."

"Actually, I do. He told me. Remember? They made him fight his friends. His family. He had to kill his own batch-siblings because that's what they promised to do for each other. I know who gave him that scar on his throat."

"Oh."

Shadow frowned. "I think I'm missing part of this story. Skye, you said he killed your batch-brothers. You never mentioned he did the same to his own."

"You had batch-siblings?" Maggie asked. "I thought you were created after the war?"

"I was. But yes, I had four brothers. They were…" Skye shook her head. "They weren't like me. They were dangerous. Violent. Experimental military models."

"And they made them fight each other." Maggie moved to Skye's side and placed a hand on her arm. "And when they went up against Striker, they died. I'm so sorry, Skye."

"They weren't right. I knew that. They were unstable and violent, but they were still my brothers. And Striker killed them."

"No," Shadow said, her voice soft. "He freed them the only way he could."

Maggie nodded. "That's what he told me. That's what his siblings promised each other. If one of them was experimented on, changed, or suffering, they wanted the others to end it for them." Maggie's heart broke at the thought of all the pain and torment her friends had lived through. "I wish…"

"Nope. Don't go there. There's nothing you could have done. We were all stuck in our own corporate hells. You, me, Skye, Striker. We couldn't save each other. We barely managed to save ourselves. Now we're together? We'll take care of each other."

"Agreed. But next time you think I need taking care of, try sending a message instead of showing up at the crack of dawn." Maggie took another long sip of her coffee and grinned. "You're always welcome, you know."

"This isn't your place, though. Will Striker want us here?" Skye asked.

"It might be. My place, I mean. We've been talking, and it seems silly for me to go to all the work of moving into my own place when I'm not even using my habi-pod right now. So for now, I think this might be where I'm living. When… if things change, I could still have my own place. Right?"

Both women nodded.

"Of course. It's yours for the asking," Shadow said.

"Thank you. That means a lot." That was good news. It meant she could enjoy her time with Striker and still have a safe place to land when it was over. That's what Haven had become for her—a safe place, full of friends who cared enough to check on her. She felt a stab of guilt. She had all this because they'd manipulated the system. Who was supposed to be here instead of her? For a moment she thought about confessing, but fear kept her silent. She couldn't go back to Earth. Not now she'd had a taste of free air and discovered what it meant to be happy. She still believed Jade had found that insurance policy she'd been looking for. Maggie had no idea what it was, but it had to be the reason Jade had gone missing.

She rubbed her wrist. Was that what Jade had sent to her implant before she disappeared? It made sense, but why would Jade send her something when she was the only person in the galaxy who knew how to decrypt it?

If she didn't find Jade soon, she'd have to figure out another way to get to that information. If Phaedra did it and the data revealed what Maggie had done, that would be the end of her life here on Haven. Striker might be able to do it, but if he knew, he'd never forgive her. Though maybe he cared about her enough to keep her secret. *Maybe.*

She still had a little time left before she had to make that choice. She'd just have to take what happiness she could find and pay the price for it later.

11

———

STRIKER CAME HOME to find Maggie putting several mugs away. He'd already done enough talking for the day, so he accessed the nearest device and broadcast his voice. "Please tell me you didn't have three mugs of coffee already this morning."

"Nope. It was *ja'kreesh*," she announced without looking at him.

"Holy *fraxx*. Tell me you're kidding. If you're not, I'm taking you to the healer right now."

"I'm joking! I had visitors already this morning. You just missed them."

"Visitors? Here? Who?"

"Yes. Yes. And to answer your last question, it was Skye and Shadow."

"Why so early?"

"Skye wanted to make sure I wasn't being held captive by some big, scary cyborg badass."

"Skye is starting to annoy me. Edge was asking about you today, too. On her behalf."

Maggie turned to face him. She was wearing his shirt,

and he felt a surge of satisfaction at seeing her in it. She was in his home, wearing his things.

"I think she'll stop now. I've assured her that you're just a big teddy bear and no threat to anything but my need to get eight hours of sleep a night."

He blinked. "You need eight hours? A night? Why didn't you tell me? And I am not a *fraxxing* teddy bear!"

"Oh. Right. Big, scary badass cyborg. Grr." She flexed her fingers into claws and made a slashing motion at the air. "I forgot."

"Brat." He folded her into his arms as she laughed and gripped the front of his shirt, pulling him down for a kiss.

Just the feel of her body pressed to his was enough to make him hard. He backed her up against the counter, letting her feel the effect she had on him.

"So… breakfast later?"

"Later," he agreed. "We've got all day."

"No, we don't. We've got traps to check. Remember? And training," she said.

"Train, yes. Traps, no. There's a security issue. They want everyone to stay close to town for the next while."

She tensed. "What happened? Skye and Shadow didn't say anything to me. Is it serious?"

"Remember when your positioning software crapped out and stranded you in the woods? Turns out, that was the start of a cascade failure. Those satellites are also part of the defense grid. They've all gone offline."

"System failure or outside interference?" There was an edge to her question but nothing more. Pride filled him. His woman wasn't one for needless panic or fear. She saw the potential problem and cut straight to the most important question.

"They're assuming it was outside interference. A team

is working to get things back online again, and the Vardarians have placed every ship they've got into a defensive position around the planet."

"How long?"

"Longer than anyone would like," he admitted. In the month since the defense grid had been activated, he'd stopped worrying so much about outside threats. They all had. In hindsight, that was a mistake.

"So, no traps today." Maggie sighed in disappointment.

"Not for you. I'll have to go out later and check them. It won't take long."

"So, I have to stay here, but you're going back into the woods? How is that fair?"

He kissed the tip of her nose. "I'm a badass cyborg. Remember?"

"I wanna be a badass, too."

"You will be. In fact, I have something that will help with that. Come."

She snickered. "I'm certainly hoping so."

Her words set his blood burning. "Soon."

First, he'd give her his gift and then they were going back to bed. If he tired her out, she'd sleep until he came back. If she really needed eight hours of rest a night… she had some catching up to do.

"Sit." He pointed to their bed. This was the one room where he always used his own voice. He wasn't sure when he'd made that decision, but it felt right.

Maggie perched on the lower corner of the bed, her feet dangling several inches off the floor. "Sitting."

"So, the trick to getting you to listen to me is to offer you presents?" He tapped the wall and a storage compartment slid out. He pulled out the *kes'tarv* he'd had made for her and turned to offer it to her. "This is yours."

"Is that what I think it is?" Maggie let out a squeal of joy and bounded off the bed. He expected her to take the weapon, but she ignored it and threw her arms around him, instead. "Thank you!"

"You're welcome."

"No. I mean it. Thank you. This is…" she looked up at him with shining eyes. "You really trust me with my own *kes'tarv?*"

"I do. And this isn't just a melee weapon." He offered it to her again.

"Holy *fraxx*. Is this like yours?" She took it and spun it in one hand.

"It is. So try not to blast a hole in anything during training."

She whooped and hugged him again. "I am going to be the baddest of badasses now." She stuck out her tongue at him. "For a human, anyway."

"You don't need to be, you know."

"Human?" she asked, confused.

"A badass. That's my job. You can just be yourself." He didn't want her to change into someone like him. She was fierce, funny, and full of life and joy. Despite everything she'd been through, she hadn't let anything dim her light.

She laughed. "I'm not sure who I *am* anymore. I know who I used to be…" Her smile vanished and her fingers tightened around the shaft of the weapon until her knuckles showed white. "Magpie."

"Isn't that a bird?"

"It was. They're extinct now. The story goes they used to steal shiny things to decorate their nests." Tension crackled off of her and she seemed to brace herself before speaking again. "I did that. I stole things. Not a lot, and never from anyone who couldn't afford it, but…"

"You were trying to survive." He gathered her back into his arms, tucking her head beneath his chin and holding her tightly. He knew what she was feeling—the guilt and recrimination. He also knew she'd forgiven him for far worse.

"I know. But I…"

"You did what you had to. We all did. I don't know who you were, Maggie Piper. I've never met this Magpie person. The woman I know danced in the sunlight within seconds of setting foot on this planet. She prepared for an uncertain future by repurposing other beings' trash, and she doesn't let anyone tell her where she can and cannot go, even when it's for her own safety."

"You saw me dancing? I don't remember you being there."

"I was in the woods. Watching."

"I should have known." She relaxed and looked up with a smile. "You've been watching over me since the day I got here."

"I guess I have. You good with that?"

"Very." She stretched up to kiss his chin. "How's your throat?"

Why would she ask about that? It took him a moment to switch mental gears. He'd spoken a lot in the last few minutes. And that wasn't the first time he'd spoken today. "It's fine. Good, actually."

"No pain?"

He took a moment to assess and was surprised to note there was no discomfort. "No."

"I'm glad to hear it. I'd hate to think that what we're about to do would cause you any pain."

"What are we doing now?"

She pulled away from him, backing up until she

reached the wall on her side of the bed. Without a word, she set down her new *kes'tarv* and then started to undress.

"I want to hear you groaning *my* name before you leave me here all alone with nothing to do but play with my new toy." She was teasing him, her voice sultry, her movements slow and sensual.

"I won't be gone long." If she kept talking like that, he'd break every speed record known to his kind to get back to her. Suddenly the idea of being stuck inside the colony for a few days didn't seem like a hardship. That's time he could spend with Maggie, either naked, training, or drinking free beers while making sure the patrons of the Bar None remembered their manners.

"You better not be." She dropped his shirt onto the floor and opened her arms to him. "Since I'll be here, waiting for you to come home."

He crossed the room in a heartbeat, sweeping her into his arms and onto the bed. *Home.* The word resonated inside him. Until Maggie, this place had been where he slept and ate while he worked on his cabin. But now she was here, it had become something else. Maybe it wasn't home yet, but it was more than it had been... and so was he.

By the time Striker set out to see to his traps, Maggie was ready to curl up in their bed and nap. Keeping up with her cyborg lover wasn't easy, but holy *fraxx*, it was worth it. He was as demanding and growly in bed as he was out of it, but he could also be surprisingly tender and sweet.

Her gaze fell on the weapon he'd given her. *Or maybe I have a skewed idea of what sweet is...*

As tempting as a nap was, she had too much to do to stay in bed. She programmed up a small cup of *ja'kreesh* with a hearty breakfast and then grabbed a quick shower while the food dispenser prepared her order.

She was halfway through her meal when her comm unit chirped a triple chime that indicated she had an urgent message. She dropped her fork and rushed back to the bedroom to see who it was from. *Jade.*

"Yes! Finally." She opened the message, her heart racing. Where was she? What the hell happened back on Earth?

To her bitter disappointment, it wasn't a video but a text message, and a short one at that.

"Magpie. Hunters coming for you. Time for little bird to fly. J."

Another coded message, all of it bad news. The codewords meant the message was truly from Jade, and Maggie needed to disappear. Now.

At least Jade was still alive. That was something. Maggie held onto that slim thread of hope as she raced around the room. She'd gotten sloppy in the last few days. Her things were scattered, the bag she normally kept packed and ready to go empty and pushed under the bed.

"Stupid," she muttered as she gathered up what she could. She knew better than to get comfortable somewhere. The universe saw it as an irresistible challenge to start throwing trouble her way. It was almost five minutes before she was ready to go.

She set down her comm and her tablet in the middle of the kitchen table and recorded a quick message. "Striker, I'm in trouble. Need to hide. Can't stay at the colony in case trouble follows me. If you want to help, I'll be with the cookies." She should have stopped the recording there, but her mouth kept moving. "And in case I don't see you again. I'm sorry. I..."

She cut herself off before the words "I love you" slipped out. She didn't. *Did she?* It was too soon... and likely too late. Not to mention the fact she didn't have time for a major emotional epiphany at the moment. She ended the recording and sent it to his comm unit. She'd leave her devices behind. It wasn't likely they could track her that way, but she couldn't risk it. She'd brought enough trouble to Haven already. Even if she didn't have a *fraxxing* clue who or what was coming for her.

As vague as she'd been, she was certain he'd understand the message. She was going to his cabin. If someone figured out where she was staying right now, they wouldn't know how to find his place in the woods. Only a handful of beings knew where it was. It was the safest place she could think of.

The cabin was on the far side of the river from her current location, which meant a long walk through the middle of the colony or a longer walk to skirt the edges and try to avoid being seen.

"Long walk it is." She shouldered her pack and headed out into the cold morning air. At least the weather suited her mood—dark, dismal, and with a threat of a storm on the horizon.

She was only halfway there when Striker caught up to her. One second she was alone in the woods and the next he was in front of her, his *kes'tarv* in his hand and his entire body singing with tension. He was panting slightly, something she'd never seen before.

"I swear I'm putting a bell on you the next time we're out here," she quipped.

He didn't even crack a smile. "Why are we out here? You're supposed to be in town where it's safe."

A ball of icy dread formed in her gut. This was it. It was time to confess. She thought they'd have more time. She bought herself a few more seconds by moving in and hugging him. Just in case it was the last time, she wanted to remember what it was like to feel warm, safe, and protected.

He held her close, curving his bigger body around hers. "Tell me what's going on so I know how to help." His voice softened. "Maggie. Who's trying to hurt you?"

"I don't know."

"Explain."

She stayed snug in his arms as she talked. "I got a message from Jade. No details. Just telling me hunters were coming and that I needed to run."

"Where is she? Why? Who would be hunting you?"

Any other time, she'd be happy to hear him speaking so much. Today, though... today every question he asked just meant the truth had to come out. This all had to be related to what she and Jade had done.

"There's something I haven't told you. Or anyone." She leaned back so she could look into his face. "I'm not supposed to be here. I cheated."

He let go of her and stepped back, his expression cold and wary. "Explain."

She told him everything. By the time she was done, he'd let go of her and moved away. It was only a few meters, but it might as well have been light years.

"You lied!" he snarled and lashed out with his bare fist. The blow snapped a nearby sapling, sending it toppling to the ground.

For the first time, Maggie saw the man Skye had

warned her about. Dangerous. Feral. Furious. "I was trying to survive. You said you understood that."

"I thought I did." He was pacing now, prowling back and forth in front of her. "But this? You've endangered everything we're building here. You brought human bullshit to Haven. I trusted you. I thought you were different, but you're not. You used us."

"I didn't know anyone would come after me."

He glowered. "Why would I believe that? You lied to all of us. You lied to *me!*"

"I didn't know this would happen. I don't know what they want. Me? Whatever Jade stuck in my arm?"

She couldn't ask him to retrieve the data right now. He was too angry at her, and he had reason to be. "Jade's the only one who can retrieve it. We have to find her."

"No." His voice was as cold as the winter wind rattling through the trees.

"No?"

"There's no we. There's just you. This is a human problem. Humans will have to fix it." Striker pointed behind her. "Go back."

"I can't. If they come for me there, innocent beings could get hurt." Which is why she'd come out here, away from everyone else.

"Now you're worried about that?" Striker snorted in angry disbelieve. "It's a little late."

"I know. And I'm sorry."

"Too late for that, too." He pointed again, back the way she'd come. "Go. It's not safe for you out here."

She wasn't sure if he meant from the hunters or him. Maybe it was both. "It won't be safe for the others if I go back."

He snarled in frustration and twisted the *kes'tarv* he

still held. It snapped to full extension. "Go back! Tell Skye and Shadow what you've done. Ask for their help. I'm done." He reinforced his words with a blow that shattered another tree trunk, sending bark and wood chips flying.

"I know you're angry. I deserve that. But I wanted…" she swallowed hard to try and push down the lump in her throat. "I'm sorry. What we had was… *fraxx*. I'm sorry I screwed up the best thing to ever happen to me. You deserved better."

She turned and bolted into the woods, hardly able to see past the tears that blurred her vision.

She ran until her lungs burned, not caring where she was going or what was in her way. Instinct must have kicked in because when she finally stopped, it only took a few seconds to recognize where she'd wound up. She was near the clearing where she'd first met Striker.

"Might as well grab my stuff while I'm here." She hadn't added to her cache of supplies in a while, but if she gathered it all up, she'd have enough. Striker had taught her how to make a simple emergency shelter in case she got lost. She could find a spot to hole up for a few days. She had food, water, a heat source, and a change of clothes. All she needed was shelter from the elements.

She checked the tree for bark spiders and then pulled out her pack and set off to her next hiding place. Striker was right. She'd brought enough trouble to Haven already. He'd been wrong about one thing, though. She needed to stay away from Haven. If she went back, she'd make everyone there a target. She'd stay away as long as she could and hope that by the time she ran out of supplies, the defense grid was back up.

Fraxx. The grid. More pieces of the puzzle fell into

place. Taking down the defense grid *had* to be connected to everything.

She froze as the full weight of that realization sank in. Someone had taken down the grid to reach her. It was her fault the entire colony was vulnerable.

Striker's words came back to haunt her. *"You've endangered everything we're building here."*

Guilt tore at her, shredding her plans to hide away until the danger was past. Striker was right after all. She'd caused this. She needed to stay and fix it.

All her instincts screamed in protest. When things went bad, she cut and run. That's what she'd always done. Vanished. Regrouped. Started again.

Only this time, there was nowhere else to go. If she left, she was walking away from her home and every friend she had left. She'd be giving it all up and becoming Magpie again.

She didn't want that.

Resolution stiffened her spine and made her turn back toward the colony. She wasn't running again. Her hand fell to the *kes'tarv* at her hip. This time, she'd stand and fight for what she wanted.

12

———

STRIKER'S ANGER swirled around him, as familiar as his favorite boots. He hadn't felt this way in a long time—not since Reamus Station. Back then he'd used his rage as fuel, letting it burn hot and bright even on his darkest days.

Time and Maggie had helped him leave some of that fury behind, but now he'd been cast into shadow again, and Maggie had sent him there. He'd trusted her…

Another sapling toppled as he lashed out with his *kes'tarv*. As it hit the ground, he had a flash of insight. Destroying trees wasn't going to solve anything. It wasn't making him feel better. He looked down at the weapon in his hand and then at the surrounding woods.

All the platitudes he'd heard since living here came rushing back, only this time, they made more sense. He *was* more than his programming. Anger and violence weren't his only choices. Feeling slightly foolish, he took several slow, deep breaths and tried to shake off the dark mood that gripped him.

To his surprise, it worked. The bright edges of his anger dimmed a little. His thoughts cleared. He twisted the grip of his *kes'tarv* and the weapon retracted into itself. Maggie had fled out of earshot, but he replayed the last few moments of sound. She was headed in the right general direction to make it back to the colony. A little off-course, but she knew these woods well enough to find her way.

Still... things weren't safe right now. He should let someone know Maggie was headed back. He activated an internal link to Skye. *"I hear you were at my place this morning because you were worried about Maggie."*

"I'm sorry I misjudged you," Skye replied.

"I'm not the only one you misjudged. Maggie fooled us all." He summarized things for Skye.

"So that's what she was hiding."

"You knew?" he demanded.

"About the cheating? No. And I didn't know about her past until today. Shadow told me after we left your place. Shadow had every human colonist carefully vetted before they were allowed to make the journey. The lottery wasn't nearly as random as I thought it was."

"Shadow deliberately brought a thief to Haven? Why the fraxx would she do that?"

"I asked the same thing. She said Maggie and her friend Jade were both excellent candidates. They're resourceful, determined, and smart."

"And they cheated to get here."

"That's new information and we'll have to address that. But she's not the first to manipulate the system to get here."

"Who else?"

"Every cyborg here," Skye reminded him.

"River did that. I was locked in a cryo-pod because you and the others told the humans we were too dangerous to be woken up." He'd been forced into a pod by his captors with no

idea if or when he'd ever regain consciousness. When he woke again, he was here, bound by rules he hadn't agreed to. Haven was their sanctuary, but it was also their prison. None of the cyborgs here were allowed to leave. They had fewer rights than even the rest of their kind.

"And because River and her allies forced Torex Mining Corporation's hand, we're free."

"Not entirely."

"Would you rather be back on Reamus?"

He growled. *"Never."*

"Me either." Skye was silent for a moment. *"You said Maggie was on her way here. I should set out and meet her on the bridge and make sure she's okay."*

"She wasn't at my place. I found her in the woods. She thought she could hide at my cabin. I sent her back to the colony."

"So, you and she are both out in the woods right now despite the danger?"

"For the moment."

"You two are a lot alike."

The comment made him smile and then scowl. *"I'm nothing like her."*

"If you really believe that, you need to book some time with our new counselor… once she gets here."

"Not happening. I'm fine. Happy. Sane." He looked around at the trees he'd broken in his anger. So, maybe not happy. The only time he'd ever truly felt that was when he was with Maggie. Maggie, who had lied to him.

Maggie… who should have made it back to the colony by now.

He was on the move before he even thought about what he was doing. He followed her trail easily. Her boot prints were still fresh and clear on the path. If she'd followed it, she would have wound up near one of the outer bridges, an easy walk away from the human area of Haven.

Now she was headed for… He took a moment to get his bearings. *Veth.* She wasn't on her way to the colony. If she kept going in this direction, she'd end up at one of her caches.

"You went quiet. What is it?" Skye asked a few seconds later.

"I don't think she's going back. I'll find her and bring her to you myself. No way can she survive out here without proper shelter. She's only human." An unenhanced, soft, stubborn female who was determined to risk her own life if it meant keeping danger away from the rest of the colony. Dammit. She'd said as much, but he'd been too angry to listen.

"Find her. Please?" Skye asked, her voice barely more than a whisper in his head.

"On my way. I know where she's going. I'll contact you again when we're on our way back." He set off at a ground-eating lope, keeping an eye out for signs of her passage in case he'd been wrong about her destination.

"You're not going to hurt her. Are you?"

Skye's question made him flinch. *"Never."*

"It's just… you're angry. I've seen what you can do when you're like this."

Something broke deep inside him and a torrent of truth poured out. *"I'm sorry about your batch-siblings, Skye. But you need to understand something. What I did to them wasn't out of rage. It was the only way I could end their suffering. Back then, I was angry almost all the time."*

"I remember. You were terrifying."

"I'm sorry about that, too." His rage had kept him alive,

but it also isolated him, keeping everyone else away. At the time, he'd wanted it that way.

"The only time I wasn't angry was when they made me fight."

"But you…" Skye didn't finish.

"I killed them. Yes. But never in anger. All I felt inside that cage was grief."

Skye was quiet so long he thought she might have disconnected. *"I didn't know. I'm so sorry."*

"Don't be. We all had a role to play in that hellish place. We did what we had to do."

Maggie's words echoed inside his head. *"I was trying to survive. You said you understood that."*

Guilt, regret, and remorse sank their claws into his heart. "I'm an asshole," he said aloud and then switched to his internal channel. *"I'll message you when I find her."*

"Stay safe. I have a bad feeling about all this."

He didn't disagree. He needed to find Maggie and get her back to the colony… just as soon as he apologized. That needed to be done first because no way was he going to let anyone else overhear that conversation. He'd already done enough damage to his reputation today.

When he reached the little clearing, it was empty. The bloodvine had been cleared from her usual path, which meant she'd already been and gone. Which way, though?

He started walking the edge of the space and found her outgoing tracks. It looked like she was heading back to Haven. Why was she heading for the colony if she was planning on hiding in the woods? It didn't make sense.

Still, her tracks were clear enough. He followed, relieved she'd come to her senses.

His relief was short lived.

Less than two minutes later the bottom fell out of his

world. The scent of scorched wood hung on the air, the trees around him marked with blaster impacts. The underbrush had been trampled almost flat in some spots, and he counted at least three pairs of boot prints too large to be Maggie's.

Fear and fury churned in his guts as he took it all in. Maggie's tracks were the only ones leading to this point. That meant the others had either flown or ridden some kind of hover-transport.

He saw a patch of trampled bloodvine in the undergrowth. Some of the thorns still had blood on them. Whoever had walked through it hadn't known to move it out of the way first. Everyone in Haven knew how to deal with the thorny plant, which meant someone who didn't know their way around this place had taken Maggie.

Who were they and where had they gone? There were no more tracks to follow. No clues as to which way they'd fled. How was he going to find her?

He pulled his *kes'tarv* from his belt and opened it. He felt better once he had it in his hand. He twirled it, thinking about the damage he'd do once he found the bastards who'd taken Maggie.

She'd fought back. That was clear. The only energy weapon she had was the *kes'tarv* he'd given her. Had she taken down any of her attackers? He couldn't tell. But three against one were impossible odds for someone like her, even if she was armed.

Armed. With a weapon he'd given her. And it had a tracking beacon.

It took him a few seconds to activate the link. Belatedly he realized Maggie didn't know about it. He'd intended to show her this afternoon during their training session. She wouldn't be happy he'd forgotten to tell her, but he could add that to the list of things he needed to apologize for—right after he killed everyone involved in her abduction.

The tracker pinged. The simple system didn't rely on satellite support. All it gave him was a direction and relative distance to target.

Whoever had her was fleeing toward the ocean. He turned and followed, but within a minute he knew it was hopeless. The beacon pulsed every thirty seconds, and by the time the third ping came, it was clear they were traveling too fast for him to catch them. That confirmed it. They weren't Vardarians or cyborgs. Neither species could sustain that kind of speed for so long.

Strangers were on his planet, and they'd taken Maggie. Now, he was going to get her back.

He pulled out his comm unit and sent a message to the only beings he knew would come help without running afoul of the council—Wreckage and Ruin. He couldn't ask Edge or any of the others. They needed to stay and protect Haven in case he was wrong.

He had no idea how many they'd be up against, though, so he sent another message. He didn't know if Damos and Tra'var would help or not, but he didn't know who else to ask.

Then he contacted Skye. *"Someone took her. I'm going to get her back. Keep the others safe. Don't tell Edge or Shadow what's going on. They'd have to tell the council, and I don't want anyone telling me I can't go after Maggie."*

He snorted to himself. Granted, once they did know, the council would probably want to have a meeting to discuss their options. By the time they'd decided, Maggie would be safely at home. It was clear to him now that she was going to need a bodyguard... probably for the rest of her life. He was just going to have to convince her that he was the one for the job.

Once she'd forgiven him for letting his anger and biases blind him to the truth.

"Ow." Maggie's head felt like someone had used it for batting practice, and when she tried to open her eyes, only one of them did. The light made her wince. Where was she and what the hell had happened to her?

"Too bright," she mumbled and then raised a hand to touch her face. At least, that was what she wanted to do. That's when she discovered her hands were bound together in front of her. She cracked open her good eye again and took a proper look around. Metal floor. Metal walls. The hum of a fan. The familiar taste of recycled air. Haven had an atmosphere, so there was no need to recycle it. She must be on a ship. But whose? And how had she gotten here? The last thing she remembered was…

It took her still-scrambled brain a while to dredge up her memories and string them together in the right order. Once she did, she groaned and closed her eye again.

So much for being a badass. She'd done more damage to the trees than her attackers. Not that she'd had much of a chance to fight back. The transports they drove had been almost silent, and they'd surrounded her before she even realized she wasn't alone.

She'd done her best, but too much adrenaline and not enough time learning how to wield her new weapon had resulted in a short, ugly fight that had ended when something hit her in the head. There'd been a flash of red and white light and then she was falling. She'd been out before she hit the ground, and judging by how much she ached, no one had caught her on the way down. *Assholes.*

No one appeared to be around, so she eased herself slowly to a sitting position, discovering new bruises as she struggled to keep her balance with her hands bound and her head spinning.

"You look like crap." The voice was weak but familiar.

"Jade?" Maggie whipped around and nearly fell on her face as the motion triggered another bout of dizziness.

"Present. Mostly." Her best friend was in the cell across from her, and she looked like hell. Her face was gaunt, her golden skin far too pale, and she had on a disposable ship's jumpsuit that was torn and stained.

"I've missed you so much." Maggie's throat tightened and tears welled up as she took in Jade's appearance. Her bruised eye stung as the tears seeped through her swollen lids. "Oh, *fraxx*. What did they do to you? Are you okay?"

"Honestly?" Jade raised her arms from her lap. Not far, just enough for Maggie to see they were both covered in bloodstained bandages. "Not really. They took…" Jade whimpered softly and cradled her injured arms close to her body.

They'd taken her implants, and they hadn't been gentle about it. Maggie had to swallow hard to push the contents of her stomach back where they belonged. "Those bastards. We'll fix this. You're going to be okay, Jade. I promise. I'll make this right."

"Not your fault. Mine. Got sloppy. Got caught." Jade managed a crooked little smile, but all Maggie could see was the pain etched into the lines around her friend's mouth and the shadows in her eyes.

"Is this about…" Maggie raised her bound hands and dropped her gaze to the arm with the implant.

"Insurance," Jade confirmed. "I'm sorry. I shouldn't have sent it to you. Now you're *fraxxed*, too."

"Can they hear us right now?"

Jade nodded firmly but said, "Nope."

Damn. So much for just being able to say, "Don't worry. Help will come." Striker was angry at her, but he'd sent her back because he wanted her safe. When he discovered she wasn't there, he'd come looking. At least, she hoped he would. She'd screwed things up between them, but even if he didn't come himself, he'd tell Skye and Shadow what she'd done… and they'd want to look for her.

Unless they decided she was more trouble than she was worth. No. They wouldn't do that to her. She had friends here—beings who cared about her.

"Family," she whispered the word to herself. She had a family. And she'd let them down. Striker was right. She'd brought too much of her old self to Haven. It was a mistake she wouldn't make again… if she lived through this.

"Family?" Jade asked.

"You remember that gang who came after us a while back?"

"Which one?" Jade asked and cocked a brow in question at the sudden change in topic, but she didn't say anything else. She'd caught on to what was happening. Maggie was speaking in code. Yet another thing Maggie thought she'd left behind.

"The Wilde Ones. You remember. It was about five years ago. They thought we'd targeted one of theirs and were out for revenge." The Wildes were a family, a mishmash of siblings, cousins, friends, and lovers who all claimed the same last name. If you crossed one of them, you crossed them all.

"Right. We tried to duck them for weeks but they kept hunting us down."

"And they never stopped. Not until we finally met and gave them proof we weren't the ones they were after."

"Yeah."

Maggie looked hard at Jade and then clenched her hands together and looked pointedly toward the back wall of her cell. "Family," she repeated.

Jade's eyes widened slightly and a hint of her old fire flashed in her eyes. "Too bad neither of us had any worth a damn back home."

"Truth. No one there is going to help us out of this," Maggie agreed and tried to make herself more comfortable. Jade had gotten the message. Hope wasn't lost. Not while they were still on Liberty.

"Any idea why we're not airborne yet?"

Jade flashed her a grin that was pure defiance and fire. "I warned these assholes that the grid might not stay down long. That Vardarian coding is complicated."

"Alien tech is tricky," Maggie agreed. "Can you bring it down again?"

"Not from here." Jade glanced up. "I need to be close enough to tap into the network. My implants weren't designed to reach orbital satellites. Serious oversight on the designer's part. I mean, think of the opportunities we could have had back on Earth. I was already a menace to society… I could have been the queen!"

"Queen Jade has a nice ring to it. Think there's an opening for royalty on this world?"

Jade shook her head, eyes dark and shadowed with grief. "They took that from me, Magpie. The only thing I was good at… and they tore it out of me one piece at a time."

"We'll get out of this somehow, Jaybird. The Vardarians can fix you up."

"Somehow," Jade gave her a wan smile. "Maybe. Fixing this?" she looked down at her bloodied bandages. "I don't think so."

Maggie had never seen her friend so despondent. Jade was a fighter. To see her like this hurt her heart. She cast about for something to say, but Jade beat her to it.

"How'd they finally catch you? I heard one of them complaining you were holed up in town and they couldn't figure out how to get to you without being seen. I'm glad you ignored my message to run."

Maggie frowned. "I didn't. I left five minutes after I got it. I was in the woods when they found me."

"Those *fraxxing* bastards. I sent that message days ago. Dammit, they're smarter than I gave them credit for. They must have blocked it and then sent it once they had a plan to find you."

If they knew where she was, they'd been watching her. No wonder they'd managed to find her. Once she left the colony, she'd gone to all the same places she usually did. It was inevitable they'd catch up to her.

"So, any idea who they are?"

"Assholes of the first order? Brutes that get off on hurting people who can't fight back?" Jade curled her arms closer to her stomach. "I don't know. Can we talk about something else?"

"I've missed you."

"Same. It's been weird not having anyone to talk through my plans with. What's it like here? Got an alien boyfriend yet?"

"No alien boyfriends." She wasn't going to mention Striker. She didn't want to warn their captors about him.

Not that she was sure he would come, or even if he was her boyfriend anymore, but that information was too important to share right now.

"They're nice, though. Every Vardarian I've met has been kind and helpful. They're also the most flirtatious species I have ever met. They might bond for life, but until they find their mates, they're all about enjoying themselves."

"Yeah? Sound like my kind of beings. I wish I'd gotten to meet one. Breathed some fresh air for once in my life."

"The air is amazing. The sky takes some getting used to." She told Jade all about the colony and the woods, making sure not to mention any names or important details. She didn't know what their captors were waiting for, but they'd be coming for her sooner or later. If this was all the time she had left, she'd spend it trying to comfort her friend. It also served to distract herself from the heartache that started every time she thought she might never see Striker again.

If she made it out of here, she'd make him listen to her one more time so she could come clean about everything, starting with the fact that she was falling in love with him.

She wasn't sure how much time had passed before they heard voices. Long enough she'd had to change positions twice to stop her legs from falling asleep. "It's your *fraxxing* fault we can't do the extraction easily." The male voice was clipped and angry. The second she heard it, Jade hunched into a ball and went utterly still. Maggie did the same.

"You told me to make her compliant. I did. Quit

bitching," another male voice spoke, and now she could hear them walking, coming this way.

"By ripping out her implants, which she needs to be able to pull the data. This was supposed to be a quick, clean operation."

"Still can be."

"Clean? Are you kidding me right now? The droids have been cleaning up the mess you made in the interrogation room for hours. I'm going to have to pay to get it decontaminated and resealed when we get back, and it's coming out of *your* share."

"Fine. But we can still make this quick. I can get what we need and then we're out of here."

They were close now, and Maggie risked a quick glance up. Two human males were coming down the narrow corridor, both wearing combat gear with an insignia she didn't recognize on the shoulder. Big. Fit. With dark hair trimmed very short.

They looked military but didn't sound like it. Mercenaries, maybe? Seemed likely. But mercs cost money —a lot of it. No one she knew back on Earth could afford anything close to what these men must charge.

Two pairs of boots appeared in her field of vision. "Up you get. If you're awake, you can walk."

A crack of metal on metal made her jump. "You too, Perez, up."

The second mercenary had struck the bars of Jade's cell with something. Maggie looked up and glared as she recognized what he was holding. "That's mine."

"Not anymore. Not sure how it works, yet, but this little toy is mine now." The asshole gave her a wink. "Winner gets the spoils and all that. Nothing personal."

"He says that a lot." Jade struggled to her feet. "But I'm taking this all *very* personally."

"All you had to do was cooperate." The first man shrugged. "This didn't have to be so… messy."

The other man rolled his eyes. "Seriously? Let it go already, Tanner. I said I'd pay to have it cleaned."

"Where are we walking to?" Maggie asked as she got to her feet. She still had a headache, but the dizziness had faded.

"Perez knows where we're going. We need to extract that data storage gizmo from your arm," Tanner said.

Jade moaned and shook her head slowly. "No, no, no. I did what you asked. I told you were to find her. I took down the defense grid. You don't have to hurt her. Please?"

"Since you can't extract the data yourself, that's a bit of a problem." Tanner shot a frustrated look at his nameless companion. "We need to get that thing out of her and bring it back to our employer. We've got a contract to honor. How we remove it is up to you. Give us the passcode to decrypt the file you stole, and Piper gets a dose of anesthetic before this starts. Keep holding out on us and…" Tanner shrugged, his face utterly impassive.

Son of a bitch. That's why they hadn't killed Jade yet. She was still holding out on them. Without the passcode, they couldn't verify what they had, and it sounded like they needed to do that before they could get paid.

"You're forgetting about the heartbeat issue," Jade said.

"The what?" Tanner looked confused, but the other man grunted.

"Did you even read the report I wrote up? The redhead's gizmo is powered by the flow of blood through her veins. Some kind of mini-generator tech. The power supply stops, and that thing will automatically wipe itself and shut down. No more heartbeat, no more data. It's the whole reason we had to bring her back here at all."

Maggie just nodded, pretending to confirm what was being said. It wasn't true. That kind of technology might exist, but she certainly hadn't paid for anything that advanced. They could have killed her and cut out what they needed after she was dead. Jade must have realized that and come up with a reason to keep her alive.

"*Fraxx*! Seriously? You should have said so. Timmins said it was so we could use her as leverage against Perez. How are you going to fix this?" Tanner snarled.

"Easy. We get messy. All we need to do is keep Piper alive. A body can take a lot of damage and still have a heartbeat. We hurt her enough, I'm betting Perez will be happy to tell us how to override the safeguards just so her little friend stops screaming."

Again, he turned to her and winked. "Nothing personal."

"Asshole," Jade muttered, but there was no venom in the words, only defeat.

Maggie needed to stall. She desperately hoped help was coming, but they were running out of time. "I know how to turn that off. But if I tell you, you have to let Jade go."

"Bullshit. You don't even know the passcode! She told us that much. You're just the mule. You can't even access the data you're carrying," the big man said, pointing the tip of the *kes'tarv* at her face. "You're the brawn. She's the brains."

Jade had handed her another advantage. She'd made them believe Maggie wasn't smart enough to be a problem. "That's true, but I've got enough sense to make sure I knew how to turn that thing off. I mean, what if she died and I had to get it out myself without damaging the data? Encryptions can be broken, but not if there's nothing left to work with."

"Fine. She gives up the passcode, you tell us how to get it out of you, and we'll escort you outside before we take off. Sound good?" Tanner asked.

She didn't believe him for a second. Once Jade gave up the passcode, these men would kill them and leave the bodies to be burned to ash by the thrusters when the ship took off. She pretended to consider this for as long as she dared. "Deal."

"You know, I'm starting to think you might be the smart one," Tanner said and touched his palm to the wall. The cell door unlocked, and he swung it open with a pleasant smile that didn't reach his eyes. "Let's get this over with. Shall we?"

The moment Jade was out of her cell, Maggie moved in beside her and slung a supportive arm around her waist. They leaned into each other and followed Tanner with the other man following behind them, humming to himself like he was enjoying this. Bastard probably was.

Maggie knew her lifespan could be measured in minutes now. She was adrift in a sea of regrets and hopes for a future that was slipping away, but she still clung to the hope that Striker would come for her.

Hurry. She tried to project the thought to him, even though she knew she had no way of making him hear her. It was a wish, nothing more, but one that came from her heart.

13

"WHAT DO YOU SEE?" Striker asked the moment Tra'var cleared the treetops. He'd taken the lead on this mission and no one had said a word about it. Habits and conditioning he never expected to use again came flooding back.

"Keep your wings on. Er… hold your… *fraxx* it. I have no idea what the cyborg version of that expression is, but give me a moment here. I need to get higher before I can— Aha! Found it."

"Details," Striker requested, his voice sharp.

"You were right. They've landed a ship here. Bigger than a shuttle."

Wreckage snickered. "This is what happens when you bring civilians along."

Damos spun a pure black *kes'tarv* in his hands, making the shaft hum as it wove through the air. "There is no such thing as a civilian Vardarian, *human*."

Ruin growled. "Don't call us that."

"Shut it. All of you," Striker snapped and spoke to

Tra'var again. "I need details, Tra'v. What size is the ship? What markings do you see? Where are the doors?"

"Let me rephrase. I can't see the ship. What I can see is a big ship-shaped distortion parked on the grass between the trees and the shore. Either a cloaked vessel is there, or we've got a space-time rupture in progress on our beach."

"Anyone outside?" Striker asked.

"Not that I can see. Could be hiding behind the cloaking shield, though."

"Come on back," he ordered.

Tra'var reappeared seconds later, diving into the clearing and touching down not far from where Damos stood.

"Plan?" Wreck asked.

"Tra'var and Damos, stay here and start raining hell down on them from cover. Draw them out if you can. The more of them are outside, the easier it will be to slip past them and rescue Maggie."

"That's it?" Damos grumbled. "I thought we'd have a chance to wreak a little havoc."

"Once I'm inside, you can wreak anything you want. Try to leave someone alive, though. The council is going to want answers."

"Only one survivor? I can work with that." Damos put away his *kes'tarv* and drew a pulse rifle from its sling on his back.

"Shiny." Ruin eyed the weapon with obvious appreciation.

"If I make you one just like it, will that work as an apology for calling you human?" Damos asked.

"You can make those? *Fraxx*, yes. That would be a fine apology," Ruin said.

"If we're done proving that we can all live in peace and

harmony so long as there are weapons to ogle, can we please move to the part where we kick ass and I get my woman back?"

"Right. Sorry. Priorities." Ruin clapped a friendly hand on Damos's shoulder. "We'll talk later. Drinks at the Bar None. Lowest body count pays."

"Accepted," Damos agreed.

"And witnessed," Tra'var chimed in.

A heartbeat later, the smiles and laughter were gone. Eyes hard, jaws set, weapons ready, they made their way to the shore in total silence. They were a team, moving as one, and it felt good. In this moment, he belonged with these males, all focused on a single goal. *His* goal. For the first time in his life, he was fighting for what he wanted. He was protecting his home, his friends, and a woman who was destined to drive him crazy for centuries to come.

The Vardarians took his orders literally and hit the cloaked ship with a barrage of fire that made it look as if an army lay hidden in the trees instead of just two lunatics with enough firepower between them to start a small war.

Wreck and Ruin flanked him on either side as the three of them broke cover near what they guessed was the ship's stern. They moved at superhuman speed. To unenhanced eyes they'd be nothing more than a blur.

The invaders did exactly what he'd hoped. They focused on the Vardarians firing on them. Returning weapon fire seemed to come from nowhere with the defenders still hidden behind the cloaking shield.

"They're cheating," Ruin said via their shared link.

"Once we hit the cloak, you want to even the odds?" Striker sent back.

"On it," Ruin replied.

"Wreckage, you're with me."

They barely slowed as they reached the ship and changed direction, charging into the distorted field that hid the attackers from view. Once they were through it, the view changed. Four men, likely human, had taken up defensive positions a few meters away from the ship's main doors. The cloak had been extended to give them room to move while still remaining hidden. It was not something most standard ships could do. This was definitely some kind of military vessel.

Ruin slammed into the first invader at full speed, sending the man's body flying out of the cloaked area.

A pair of almost identical battle cries came from the woods, and the covering fire stopped. Tra'var and Damos were about to join the fight, and he left them to it.

Running footsteps announced another wave of fighters leaving the ship, so he and Wreckage ducked out of sight beneath the ramp. Four more of the invaders charged out. They thought they were defending their friends. Striker knew they'd just signed their death warrants.

"Remember, there's at least one hostage inside. Be careful who and what you shoot."

"This is not my first firefight. Don't worry. I'm not going to blast your woman."

His woman. Damn, he liked the sound of that. Maggie was stubborn and beautiful with a soul as fiery as her hair… and she was *his*. Or she would be, just as soon as he got her back from the humans who'd taken her.

The first corridor they entered was empty and no automated defenses started firing on them.

"Shoddy security," Wreckage muttered softly.

Striker agreed. Whoever they were, this outfit hadn't

prepared for the possibility they'd be boarded by hostiles. It was a costly mistake… for them.

"*Fraxx* you! We had a deal," Maggie shouted, her voice loud and full of outrage.

Striker turned toward the sound in a side corridor not three meters away. He charged forward at full speed, but it felt like an eternity passed before he reached it. Every moment he expected to hear a blaster fire or Maggie's scream as something terrible happened and he lost her forever.

Not this time. He wasn't losing someone else he cared about. Not again.

Someone roared in fury, and it took him a moment to realize the sound was coming from him.

It echoed down the short hallway and bounced off several closed doors.

At the end of the corridor, one door stood open. The air reeked of cleanser and other, less wholesome smells—ones he remembered from Reamus. He shook the dark memories off and kept running. *Not again.*

Someone stepped into the doorway as he closed the last few steps. Male. Human. Dark haired. Blaster raised. That was all he had time to register before impact.

He'd never fought an unenhanced human before. He'd expected them to be knocked back and then come up fighting. That's what a cyborg would have done. This was no cyborg.

He heard a meaty sound like a wet sack of bread hitting a hard floor, and the man flew backward. With another wet smack, he hit the bulkhead on the far side of the room, and when he slid to the ground, he left a trail of blood on the wall that told Striker he wouldn't be getting up again.

"Striker!" Maggie cried out.

He turned just as another man fired at him. The shot went off target because Maggie grabbed the man's arm, but it still managed to graze his bicep. Striker shut down his pain receptors before he felt more than the first twinge of discomfort.

"Bitch!" Maggie still clung to the male's arm despite the blows he was raining down on her head and shoulders. "Let go!"

Another woman was in the room, and she flew at the man, too, but he knocked her away with a wild swing of his free arm before kicking Maggie in the stomach. Maggie sagged to the floor with a winded cry of pain.

Striker's control snapped. Cold rage flowed through him, and he came at the other man faster than a serpent's strike. He dropped his blaster and went after his target with his bare hands.

He distantly registered another blaster firing. A woman screamed, but he couldn't see who had fired or what they'd hit. He focused all his fear and fury on the man who taken Maggie from him.

He didn't stop the beating until Wreckage grabbed him by the shoulders and pulled him off. "You can stop now. He's so dead I think we're going to need a new medical definition for his condition."

"Maggie?" Striker panted.

"I'm here." Maggie flew into his arms and hugged him so hard he thought his reinforced ribs might actually break.

"He hurt you. Are you okay?"

"I am now." She looked up at him and smiled, though her eyes were full of tears. "You came."

"You're under my protection. That hasn't changed."

She made a soft sound that might have been hopeful, happy, or sad. He couldn't tell. "I wasn't sure about that."

"Be sure." He touched her cheek, belatedly realizing his hands were stained with the dead man's blood. When he tried to pull away before he sullied her skin with it, she grabbed his hand and pressed it to her face.

"I'm sorry I lied to everyone. About everything. You were right. I brought the worst parts of humanity with me to Haven."

"I'm sorry, too. I wasn't fair to you. No one here led a perfect life before they came here. Especially me."

He leaned down and kissed her, savoring the taste of her lips and the salty tang of her tears—tears she'd shed for him because she wasn't sure he'd come for her. He'd been an ass, and it had nearly cost him the one thing he couldn't bear to lose... Maggie.

"I will always protect the ones I love," he whispered against her mouth. "Always."

"Yeah?" She squeezed him so tightly he felt his ribs creak. "I love you, too. When you sent me back to Haven, I thought I'd lost my chance with you."

"And when I realized you were in trouble, I thought I'd lost you forever."

He kissed her again, adrenaline and need coursing through him like the most potent pharma in the galaxy. She was back in his arms, and he wasn't going to let her go again. Not now. Not ever.

"You're mine, now, Maggie Piper."

He expected her to argue with him or at least sass him. Instead, she uttered a delighted laugh and rose on her toes to kiss him. "Yes, I am."

~

"Holy fraxx. I leave you alone for a few weeks and you go and fall in love?" Jade demanded weakly.

"Yeah. Sorry I didn't mention it before. I couldn't tell those assholes I had a big, badass cyborg coming to rescue me. It would have spoiled the surprise."

She lowered her voice to a bare whisper only Striker would be able to hear. "And I wasn't sure you'd come."

"Always." The word was a promise that made her heart soar.

"Good." Jade managed to fix Striker with a glare that would have been intimidating if she wasn't delivering it from the floor with her injured arms cradled in her lap. "You better take care of her, big guy. She needs a keeper and I'm going to be laid up for a while."

"I don't need a keeper!"

"Really?" Jade gritted her teeth and nodded down at her leg. Maggie belatedly realized that Wreckage was crouched beside Jade, applying a dressing to her upper thigh.

"Jade! Holy *fraxx*. Your leg. What happened?"

"I took a blaster bolt for you." Her friend said with a grim smile. "I'm gonna want a medal for that."

"She threw herself right into the line of fire," Wreck looked up quickly, his expression one of admiration and surprise. "You could have died."

"Could have." Jade shrugged. "But life would be awfully boring if we never did anything that could get us killed."

Wreckage blinked and then grinned. "Oh... I like this one. Can we keep her?"

"Well, technically Jade was supposed to be one of the human colonists…" Maggie turned but didn't leave the comfort of Striker's arms. She wasn't sure when she'd be ready to do that… if ever.

"Then it's settled. She's staying." Wreckage gathered Jade gently into his arms and stood. "Ruin says it's clear outside. They're sweeping the ship now. Help is on the way. Medical support and transport home for everyone."

"Hey! Did I say you could pick me up?" Jade protested.

"No. But you can't walk. How else will you get outside?" Wreck asked.

"Don't argue, Jaybird. I've discovered that cyborgs are even more bullheaded than humans."

Striker nuzzled her ear. "I'd argue that point, but I don't want to fight right now."

"Me either."

"Oh, you're a cyborg?" Jade looked at Wreckage with interest. "And pretty, too."

She raised a hand and then dropped her arm again. All the life faded from her expression and she closed her eyes. "And I'm a broken mess. Take me out of here, please."

To Maggie's surprise, Wreckage's expression turned tender, and he leaned down to whisper something to Jade. Then, he cradled her gently in his arms and carried her out past them.

"You should get that arm looked at, Striker," he said as he left.

"Arm? What about your arm?" She twisted around until she was facing him again. High on one arm was a scorched patch of flesh and blood-soaked fabric. "Did everyone get shot in the last five minutes but me? Why didn't you say something?"

"I forgot about it. Pain's blocked for now. My medi-bots will take care of it by tonight."

"Then why did he tell you to get it looked at?"

"If I get it cleaned up, it'll heal faster."

She grabbed his uninjured hand and started pulling him toward the door. "Then that's what we're doing. Come with me."

He let her lead him for a few steps, but adrenaline and fear had made her legs shaky and she stumbled.

When Striker drew her back to him and lifted her into his arms, she didn't protest, even though she knew it couldn't be good for his arm to carry her this way.

"How about we treat you first and then worry about me?" he said.

"I'm okay." She probably had a concussion, but she wasn't going to mention that just yet.

"We'll let a trained professional make that decision."

She opened her mouth to argue, but he stopped her next words with a kiss so hot she forgot about everything else. She moaned and wrapped her arms around his neck, giving him the only thing she could—her surrender.

Heat tore through her like firestorm and she melted into his arms, leaning into his strength. It shouldn't have felt so right. Not given where they were and what they'd just gone through. Striker's hands were bloodstained and dead bodies were strewn throughout the room, but none of that mattered right now. He'd come for her. Saved her. He loved her.

That meant everything.

Striker carried her out of the room without breaking their kiss, and she fell into it eagerly. The carnage and fear were blotted out by his touch. She needed to feel safe right now, at least until she could find a way to stop thinking about how close she'd come to a painful death.

The last few minutes played out again inside her mind, but this time she had the luxury of knowing she and Jade would both survive.

She'd been inside the nightmarish room when the shooting started. Hope had buoyed her up for a moment, but then she'd seen the uneasy look on Tanner's face. He was almost out of time... and he'd known it.

"Who came for you, you little bitch? Who else is going to die today because of you?" He'd cut her hands free and shoved her into a nightmarish chair so laden with restraints her skin crawled just from sitting in it.

The one watching Jade had set aside her kes'tarv and now held a blaster to Jade's temple.

"Stop struggling or your friend dies here and now."

Maggie had frozen in place the moment the threat was spoken.

"Smart girl. Now tell me how to override the failsafe or she'll be dead in ten seconds."

With nothing left to lose, Maggie shouted, hoping someone might hear her.

"Fraxx you! We had a deal."

Someone had heard her. Striker.

He'd charged into the room like an angry god. He hadn't just stopped the men trying to hurt her. He'd destroyed them. For her.

Memory and reality folded together and she was back in the here and now, safe in Striker's arms. As they left the ship, euphoria overtook her. She threw back her head and laughed, letting the rain fall on her upturned face.

"You alright?" Striker asked, frowning.

"Wonderful. I'm free. You're here. You love me. This has been an insane day, but it's ending well."

"It's not over yet." He descended the ramp and carried her away from the others, heading for the bow of the ship.

"Where are we going?"

"Close your eyes."

"Why?"

He growled at her. "For once, will you do as your told?"

"Just this once. Since you saved my life and all." She closed her eyes, but not before she saw him shake his head and smile.

"Brat."

She stuck out her tongue and laughed.

In less than a minute he stopped walking. New sounds pressed into her awareness. A rhythmic hush-shushing noise she didn't recognize, though it felt like she should know it. The rain still fell, but the wind against her face felt heavy with moisture and carried new scents—salt and vegetation of some kind.

"Open your eyes."

She did and then squealed in delight. It was the ocean. All the way to the horizon, all she could see was water. Waves lapped the shore, hissing across the sand and then retreating again.

"It's beautiful."

"So are you. It seemed a shame to leave without letting you see the ocean first, since we're already here."

"But we can come back again soon?" She hadn't stopped staring at the view, trying to memorize as much as she could before they had to go.

"Soon," he promised.

"Then take me back to the others. I want to check on Jade."

To her surprise, Striker chuckled. "She's fine. Both Wreck and Ruin are giving me updates."

"They are? Why?"

"Because I asked them to. I knew you'd want to know how she was doing. Apparently she is fascinating, stubborn, and resistant to common sense. Sounds like someone else I know."

"I have no idea who that could be."

"You should. She's the woman I love." He bowed his head and kissed her tenderly.

"Oh, her. Yeah, she's a lucky woman." She stroked her hand down the back of his neck and kissed him back. She already knew she'd remember this moment forever. It wasn't just her head that would hold on to this memory. Her heart would, too.

"Ready to go home, brat?" he asked several slow kisses later.

"I am."

"And just so we're clear. It's our home, now. Not mine. Ours. You're not safe on your own, so I'm not going to let you out of my sight."

She laughed again as he turned and started carrying her back to the others. "Okay. But that means we're going to need more furniture."

"Whatever you need. But you have to promise me something first."

She tensed. "What?"

"Whatever we buy, it stays in the house or the cabin. No more stashing things in the woods."

"But what if things go sideways?"

"Then we stay and fight for our home." He kissed the

tip of her nose. "But we make sure the cabin has plenty of supplies. Just in case."

"Just in case," she agreed. She wouldn't need to hide caches anymore. That part of her life was over. No more running. No more hiding. To her, that was the real definition of freedom.

STRIKER HADN'T EVEN BEEN aware that Haven had a medical shuttle until it set down not far from their little band. It had barely settled on the ground before the side door slid open and two older Vardarians jogged out followed by a silver-skinned female who stayed to set up a staging area outside the shuttle. He recognized one of them immediately. Tariq A'Nir was the colony's lead healer and had spent time taking care of the cyborgs after they woke from cryo-stasis. Both males wore sky-blue *harani*. The armbands showed their mated status. The color indicated they were both in mourning for their mate. The other male must be Tariq's *anrik*.

More Vardarians flew in while the forest was suddenly filled with the hum of dozens of air-bikes.

"Why is the whole colony here?" Maggie asked.

"Because one of our own was in danger."

Maggie nodded silently, but he saw the glimmer of tears in her eyes before she dashed them away with a swipe of her hand. He knew how she felt. He spotted Wreckage and Ruin still with Jade while Damos and

Tra'var stood guard over their prisoner—the last surviving member of the ship's crew. They'd all dropped everything when he'd asked them to. It was a humbling reminder that despite his best efforts to push everyone away, he'd made friends here.

He nodded to the two Vardarians as he moved past them, careful to keep Maggie well out of the man's reach. Not that the prisoner looked like he was much of a threat. He was younger than Striker had expected, his expression dazed as he held a hand over his still-bleeding lip. As far as Striker could tell, it was the only injury the kid had. Whoever he was, he hadn't put up much of a fight.

The two male healers were already with Jade, so Striker walked over to the medical shuttle and nodded to the silver female. "Maggie was taken prisoner. See to her."

"Vixi?" Maggie waved at the Vardarian. "I haven't seen you around lately."

"I've been helping Shadow plan for the next set of colonists and keeping an eye on my fathers." Vixi nodded toward the two male healers. "They tend to get lost in their own world when I'm away too long."

"Those are your dads? I didn't realize." Maggie wriggled in Striker's grasp. "And I'm not the one you need to look at. Striker got shot. Can you make sure he's healing okay?"

Vixi smiled. "How about I check you both at the same time? You can set her down over there, Striker, and I'll get her scanned while I take a look at your injury. And it's nice to meet you. Shadow says you've been watching over our resident rebel."

"Hey!" Maggie protested. "I'm not a rebel."

Vixi arched one blonde brow. "If you say so."

"She prefers the term brat."

Maggie rolled her eyes. "I do not."

He ignored her and set her down on one of the flat tables that had extended from the side of the ship. "Slick setup."

"Nanotech can only do so much. It's best to be prepared for the worst. Just in case," Vixi said and then turned her attention to Maggie. "Lie back, get comfortable, and don't move until I tell you to. The scan won't take long. While you do that, I'll look at Striker's injury."

"It's fine. My medi-bots can deal with it."

Vixi fixed him with a stare that would give a *gharshtu* a headache. "Sit. Shirt off. Don't argue."

Maggie snickered. "You tell him, Vix."

"No moving, Maggie. That includes your lips," Vixi kept her gaze locked on him as she scolded her other patient.

Striker decided to give in gracefully. "Where would you like me to sit?"

The female's expression immediately softened in a warm smile. "The bed next to Maggie will be fine."

The examination didn't take long. "It's healing well, but I think I can speed the process up by a day or so."

"A day?" he asked.

"The blast tore away a fair amount of muscle tissue. It will take time for your medi-bots to replace it. I can fill the wound with an organic lattice that will act as a temporary bandage and give the nanotech something to use as a framework. The lattice will dissolve and be absorbed into your system over the next week or so."

He knew nothing about this technology, but if it sped up his healing time, he was all for it. "Do it." It took him a second to remember to add, "Please."

"Happy to. Are you already blocking the pain?"

"Yes."

"Okay. Keep that up for at least two more hours if you can. After that, you should be fine with just a mild pain-blocker."

She got to work, her touch light and efficient. As she placed a light bandage over the area, she said. "I was under the impression you were mostly nonverbal. Has that changed, or is it just because you're blocking the pain right now?"

"Things have changed."

Vixi nodded. "I'm glad to hear it. Come see me in four days so I can make sure the lattice did its job and I'll do a scan of your throat at the same. Make sure everything is working properly."

He started to shake his head, but Maggie chimed in before he could. "He'll be there."

"Glad to hear it because I'm going to want to see you too, Maggie."

"Why? I'm fine."

"You are not. You have a concussion and several bruised ribs along with a few other minor bumps and bruises. Since you don't have medi-bots yet, you're going to need to take it easy for a few days." The healer held up an injector. "But you're getting a dose of healing accelerant and a pain-blocker before you leave."

"She'll be there," he confirmed. Maggie was hurting. She had no way to heal herself and no way to block the discomfort. He'd let his anger guide his decisions, and she'd paid the price. That would not happen again.

"You're both cleared for light activity. Nothing too strenuous. If there are any problems, message me. I'm listed in the colony's directory."

"Thanks, Vixi." Maggie tried to hop off the table, but

Striker got to her first, blocking her with his body and then gathering her back into his arms.

"You've got a head injury. You're not walking anywhere."

"I'm fine!" she argued.

Vixi snorted. "Your definition of fine needs work. If Striker wants to carry you, let him. But if you keep wiggling you're going to aggravate his wound."

Maggie went instantly still. "Sorry."

Striker winked at Vixi. "You're good at this."

"I get plenty of practice." She nodded toward her fathers.

They had Jade resting comfortably on a stretcher now, her eyes closed and limbs relaxed. Whatever they'd given her had knocked her out, which was probably for the best. Like Maggie, Jade had no way to shut off the pain.

"Can we go home now?" Maggie asked as soon as they were out of Vixi's hearing.

"Not just yet." He'd spotted Phaedra's bright pink hair and was already making for her position. The rest of the council were likely to be nearby. He needed to have a word with them.

He sensed it the moment Maggie realized where he was going. She tensed in his arms. "Shit. Do we have to? Now?"

"Now."

"What if they say I have to leave? What happens to us?"

"Nothing. You're not leaving."

"You can't be sure of that. What I did…"

"You are not leaving me." He had a plan, and he was going to make it work.

"Never," she murmured and kissed the corner of his mouth. "You're stuck with me."

"Damn right."

The council members were chatting amongst themselves, no doubt trying to make sense of what they'd learned and figure out what to do next. They quieted as he approached, Phaedra's mates taking up protective stances on either side of the little human. Striker ignored their posturing.

"Maggie, are you okay?" Phaedra pulled out of Tyran's hold and ran over to them.

"Apparently I have a concussion. I'll be fine in a few days. Jade's in worse shape. You won't let them send her away. Will you? At least not until she's better?"

"I talked to her briefly." Phaedra patted her arm. "She's staying right here so she can get the best help we can offer." Then she stepped back and looked at the rest of the council. "Right?"

Raze snarled something, but Sevda stepped in front of him, one hand on his chest, her other arm cradling their infant daughter. "Oh, stop. Or do I need to remind you that when I arrived, you had no legal right to even be *on* this planet?"

"I had every right," Raze argued, but his expression softened the moment he looked at his wife.

"Please. If I hadn't come along, this place would be nothing but a dust cloud by now, and you with it." Sevda smiled at Maggie. "Ignore him. He grumbles a lot, even for a cyborg."

"I know how that is." Maggie patted Striker's cheek. "It's cute. Isn't it?"

"I am not cute," Striker muttered through gritted teeth.

"Right. Sorry. Forgot again. You're a big, scary badass

cyborg. Grr." Her smile was like a supernova, lighting up his world.

"And don't you forget it." He bowed his head to kiss her gently.

She kissed him back, her hands framing his face as she gazed up at him with a look that made him feel like he was the center of her whole universe. "You saved me today. I will never forget that. You aren't just a badass, Striker. You're *my* badass. My sexy cyborg champion."

"Damn right I am. Always." He looked up to find the rest of the council smiling at them. "Maggie was hurt today. She'd heal faster if she had the medi-bot treatment."

"Six months," Skye reminded him. "She needs to be here six months before that happens. I already bent the rules enough setting her loose in the colony early."

"Not if she's claimed as the mate of a colonist."

"That clause was intended for Vardarians who experienced the *sharhal* after finding their mate," Zanyr pointed, his wings shifting slightly in agitation. "The mating fever comes on fast and creates a driving need to bite and bond with our *mahaya*. The transfer of nanotech is part of that process."

Striker nodded to the Vardarian farmer. "That's true. But there's more to it." He shifted his gaze to Denz. "You keep saying there are no sides here. That we're all one community. If so, the mating clause applies to everyone equally. Either we're all full citizens of this colony or we're not."

The prince frowned. "We are all equal here."

"Then prove it. Give Maggie the medi-bot treatment and recognize her as my mate."

"Uh, hold up. Aren't you forgetting something?" Maggie asked.

He looked down to find her glowering up at him, though the smile on her lips told him whatever he'd overlooked, she wasn't really unhappy about it. "What?"

Every female present laughed softly, and even the baby cooed and babbled at the noise.

"What?" he asked again. What was obvious to them?

"Did you forget to mention this plan to Maggie?" Denz asked, grinning.

"I'm pretty sure you're supposed to be on one knee for this, too," Maggie informed him.

"That is a human tradition. We're starting a new one. No one kneels." He set Maggie down in front of him and took her hands in his. "I love you. I promise to protect you, always. Do you love me?"

"Yes. I love you. Even if you're the most difficult, stubborn cyborg in existence."

He pulled her in and kissed her.

Cheers, applause, and catcalls erupted all around them, but he ignored everyone until he was ready. Then, he raised his head and announced, "It's decided. You're my mate."

"And you're mine," Maggie added.

"I'll see to it a vial of the medi-bots is delivered to your place immediately," Denz said. "Unless anyone has an objection they'd like to make?"

Every single member of the council smiled and shook their heads.

Striker exhaled softly. He hadn't been sure that would work, but it was the best plan he had to make sure Maggie was allowed to stay. Now, she was a full member of the colony in every way that mattered, and she was *his*.

"Thank you. All of you. You just proved that Haven

truly is a community where everyone is equal and we all have the same goals."

Edge snorted. "For a guy who doesn't talk much, you make very pretty speeches. You keep that up and I'll nominate you to take my spot on the council."

"Don't you *fraxxing* dare. I've got enough to do already." More than enough, in fact, but that was a conversation for another time.

"And the first thing I need you to do is get this data out of my arm." Maggie nodded to her wrist. "Please. Then send the file to Phaedra. I don't know what's on it, but whatever it is, those mercenaries were hired to retrieve it."

"Then let's get it out of you so you're not a target anymore." He pressed a hand to her wrist, extending his cybernetic senses to prod at the implant. It was laughably simple, and it only took him a few seconds to extract the files.

"Do you know the passcode?" he asked.

"I don't. Jade does, though." Maggie looked at Phaedra. "You talked to her. Did she give it to you?"

Phaedra grinned. "She did. Striker. Try m-a-g-3-1-4."

Striker groaned. "Seriously?"

"Afraid so."

Maggie frowned. "Now I'm the one who feels like they're missing something."

"Magpie. Mag-Pi. The first three numbers of pi are three point one four," he explained as he gathered up the data and sent it directly to Phaedra's implants.

Phaedra cocked a dark pink brow as the info registered on her end. "You have some interesting talents, Striker. I had no idea."

Braxon, her second mate, rumbled a low growl of warning. "What did he do?"

"Extracted Maggie's file with a touch and then sent it to me without even needing a direct connection."

"I made my own."

Braxon snarled. "Do not directly connect with my *mahaya* again."

"Stop it. It was a data transfer. That's all." Phaedra rolled her eyes. "He's Maggie's mate. I'm yours. No need to get growly."

"Mine," Maggie repeated with a nod. "And if we're done here, I'd like to check on Jade and then take my mate home, to our house."

"One more thing before you go." Damos strode over and held out his hand. In it was Maggie's *kes'tarv*. "I believe this is yours."

"Thank you! With everything else going on, I forgot to get that back from the asshole who took it from me." Maggie took it from him happily and then stopped and looked more intently at Damos. "Wait. How did you know this was mine?"

"Because he's the one who made it for you. Maggie, meet Damos. Damos..." Striker grinned. "My *mahaya*, Maggie."

"Those must be some amazing cookies." Damos nodded and cracked the faintest of smiles. "Congratulations. May you both be carried high by the winds of good fortune."

"Thank you. And thank you for returning this to me. It's an amazing weapon, even if it didn't help me much today."

Damos cocked a brow. "It saved your life. How else do you think we reached you in time? If Striker hadn't asked me to add a tracking beacon to your weapon..."

Fraxx. He hadn't gotten around to mentioning the tracker yet.

"Beacon?" Her brows almost vanished into her hair.

"Direction and distance only. In case you got lost again," he explained.

She mulled that over for a few seconds, but her eyes were sparkling with laughter the whole time. "As my official protector, I suppose that's acceptable."

"Protector and *mate*," he reminded her.

"Yeah. I like the sound of that." She settled deeper into his arms. "Let's go home. I need food, a shower, and you." She winked at him. "Not necessarily in that order."

He didn't bother to say goodbye to anyone. He just turned and made for the hover-bikes and transports parked near the trees.

"Take mine. Red. On the left." Edge sent him via internal link.

"Thanks."

It was time to take Maggie home.

She spent the short ride back to Haven snuggled against Striker's chest as he wove the hover-bike through the trees at dizzying speeds. She barely saw the bridge as they flew over it, and before long they were outside Striker's home. No—she corrected herself—their home.

This day had been one major upheaval after another. Decisions and consequences lined up like a ruthless parade that had nearly cost her everything. Yet, somehow, she'd made it out the other side, and so had everyone she cared about. She still had Striker, Jade, and Haven. There was still work to do and a lot of trust to rebuild, but she was getting a second chance. It was more than she expected. Hell, it was more than she deserved.

"You okay?" Striker helped her off the bike.

"More than. Just thinking about how much I have to be grateful for right now. You saved me more than once today. First from those merc assholes, and then from the council." She gripped his hand tightly enough he stopped walking and looked down at her with concern.

"What is it?"

"If what you did… what you said. If claiming me as your mate was just to protect me from the council, I need to know that. Are you sure this is what you want? That *I'm* what you want?"

His lips curled back in a silent snarl that made her want to dance for joy. If he was annoyed, he'd meant every word he'd said.

She threw herself into his arms with a wild whoop of happiness. "You *do* want me!"

"As if there was any doubt." He lifted her high in the air and then brought her in close for a kiss. "I love you. I told you that already. Why would you have any doubts?"

"Because I'm not used to having things go well for me. Plus, I don't have perfect recall and playback abilities. So I'm going to need you to remind me that you love me, okay."

"Humans…" he sighed. "So many flaws."

She stuck her tongue out at him. "But you love me anyway."

"Yes, brat. I do." His next kiss didn't stop until she was pressed up against the outer wall of his house. His lips were hard and demanding, his tongue dancing with hers as he ground the hard ridge of his cock against the seam of her pussy.

"Love you. Need you," she whispered as tendrils of fire raced through her blood and sent her heart racing.

"Soon." He had one arm outstretched and it took her a dazed moment to realize he was blindly feeling his way to the mailbox.

"Mail? Now?"

"Special delivery," he told her as he pulled something out.

"No way. Already?"

"Drones are wonderful things." He held up a slender box. "Ready?"

"Oh yes. For that. For you. For everything to come."

"Me too."

They moved inside, kissing and touching, hands flying as they tore at each other's clothes. She needed to feel him skin to skin with her. They made their way to the shower, leaving a trail of bloodstained clothes behind them. She'd send them to recycling later. They might still be useful, but she never wanted to wear anything from this day ever again. For once, she'd be a little wasteful.

Somewhere ahead of them she heard the shower start. Striker must have tapped into the house system. "Extra steam?" she asked.

"Just the way you like it."

She was surprised and pleased to note he wasn't using the system's speakers to talk to her. In fact, he'd been talking to her directly all day.

So much had changed, and somehow, it was all for the better. Feeling like she'd won the galaxy's richest lottery, she bounded into the shower and spun beneath the cascade of hot water, laughing and almost drunk on joy and need.

Striker followed her in, watching her with bemusement as she capered and danced.

"Happy?"

The water streaming down washed away the tears that fell as she turned and nodded. "So happy I don't know what to do with myself. This is all..." She spun around again, sending water flying in all directions.

"I have everything I ever wished for. Do you have any idea how amazing that is?"

He laughed and caught hold of her as she spun, dragging her into his arms. "I might have some idea, yes."

She slid her hands up Striker's broad chest to his shoulders and drew him down so she could kiss him. Fragrant steam swirled around them, the caress of the water blending with the touch of his hands as his mouth found hers.

Passion was tempered with tenderness, the passion between them building slowly as they took turns scrubbing every trace of the day's events from each other's bodies. They mirrored each other's actions, sliding soapy hands over their head and then shoulders. When he reached her breasts, she arched herself into his hands and moaned, her fingers teasing his nipples until he growled her name.

It might have been a warning, but she took it as a challenge. She loved hearing him growl at her. She smoothed her hand down the hard ridges of his stomach, laughing softly as he flexed for her.

"Any lower and you know what's going to happen," he warned her with just enough rumble in his voice to tell her he wanted her to keep going.

"We go from getting clean to getting down and dirty?"

"Very, very dirty." He caught her chin in his hand

before tipping her head so she was looking at him. Then he moved his hand so he shielded her face from the falling water. "I will take you here and now. Up against that wall."

A bolt of pure lust slammed through her at his words and she lowered her hand until her fingertips brushed over the head of his cock. "The tile will be cold," she murmured. "Maybe we should take this to the bed—"

She didn't get a chance to finish her sentence before he had her off the ground and pressed to the wall. She let go of his cock and wrapped her arms around his neck. "Do you want something from me?"

"Brat, you know what I want."

She kicked her feet gently, letting her toes bump against his calves. "I'm not sure…"

Striker didn't say a word. He just rocked his hips against her, the thick head of his cock barely brushing against the lips of her pussy.

"Oh!" She raised her legs and draped them around his hips. "Does my big, badass cyborg want to fuck me?"

"Always," he murmured. "But right now, I also want to make love to my mate."

His words made her tremble and tears of joy welled up in her eyes yet again. "I want that, too. I want you, Striker. Always."

His next kiss was tender and sweet, but it was also intense. Every part of him was focused on her, and she basked in the feeling. It was like her first day here, standing under the light of a new sun and feeling like anything was possible.

He savored her, tasting and teasing with a single-mindedness that left her quivering and half out of her mind with need. She bucked her hips and his cock slipped a little deeper into her folds. It was good, but it wasn't enough.

"You know what I want…" he whispered.

He wanted her surrender, and she was happy to give it to him. "I'm yours, Striker. All of me. I love you." She grinned. "Now, fuck me already."

"Brat!" He punctuated his statement by lifting her a little higher and rolling his hips so he slid into place at her entrance. Her toes curled as he eased himself inside her, his mouth finding hers again as they came together.

This wasn't fucking. She knew that the moment he kissed her. This was something she'd never experienced before. Every moment of pleasure was heightened by her emotions, the two of them moving as one with bodies and hearts intertwining. This was intimacy at its purest, lifting her up to heights she'd never imagined. For the first time in her life, she wasn't afraid of falling. Not when she had Striker around to catch her.

Every thrust of his hips pushed her closer to orgasm, his thick cock stroking her inner walls as he buried himself to the hilt inside her again and again.

The sounds of their lovemaking echoed off the tiled walls. The slap of wet flesh, his broken groans of need blending with her soft cries of pleasure until it felt like they were standing at the heart of their own personal storm.

She flexed her body around his, milking his cock as he drove himself into her. He groaned so she did it again, the action pushing them both to the edge of their control. His fingers tightened their hold on her hips and his thrusts sped up as he spoke her name over and over again.

Her orgasm hit like a comet strike, shattering her into a thousand pieces of perfect, shimmering bliss. Her senses were still reeling as Striker came hard, driving into her one last time before emptying himself inside her.

She slumped against him, letting him hold her up as the water poured over them. She had everything she'd ever dreamed of and more. Free air, fresh water, wide open spaces, and the love and protection of the most amazing man on any world.

She was *home*.

EPILOGUE

STRIKER TRIED to pay attention to what was being said at the meeting, but it was no easy feat with Maggie's hand on his thigh. She kept moving her fingers in slow circles that were a lot more interesting than anything the council members had to say. He was recording it and would play it back later. Not that most of it pertained to him, anyway. He was only here because Phaedra had reviewed the data files Maggie carried and was ready to tell the council what she'd found.

Phaedra finished her security report. "The defense grid is now fully functional again, and with Jade's help we've identified the weak parts of the code and strengthened them. We're also adding proximity sensors to every satellite. Anything getting close enough to make a connection will trigger an alert here in Haven."

Maggie's fingers stilled at the mention of her friend. Three days later, Jade was still in the medical bay, recovering from her ordeal. Her injuries were more extensive than he'd realized. The removal of her implants was done so brutally it had permanently damaged her nerves and muscles. Some were being regrown, and others would be replaced with neural implants. There was nothing they could do to replace the cybernetic implants she'd lost. Her body had endured too much trauma.

He couldn't imagine the pain she'd experienced or what it would be like to lose a part of himself that way. Maggie was worried about her friend, but Striker believed once she was done mourning the loss of her old self, Jade would find a way to move forward. She was too strong to do anything else.

"If there are no questions about the grid, I think it's time we moved on to the next issue," Phaedra said, still standing.

"Please. I want to know what was in that file that was so *fraxxing* important they were willing to take down our entire network to get it back," Edge stated, his eyes locked on Maggie and his tone as cold as the vacuum of space.

Maggie leaned a little closer to Striker, her fingers tightening on his thigh.

"Cool your boosters. You're scaring Maggie." He sent the reminder to Edge via a private channel.

"Sorry. Just pissed."

"Be pissed. Just don't glare at my mate at the same time."

He covered Maggie's hand with his. Tomorrow they'd both see Vixi for a checkup. Once Maggie had a clean bill of health, they'd be making an appointment for her to have the translation matrix and internal comms installed. She'd be able to speak to any cyborg in the colony once that was done, as well as the two of them having a private channel.

Phaedra tossed something from her tablet to the holographic display in the middle of the table and a short list of words appeared.

"What's that?"

"A list of names." Phaedra gestured, and the words increased in size until they were easily read from anywhere in the room. "I'm on that list," Maggie said softly.

"Everyone who came here with you from Earth is on this list. Jade showed me what she did to increase the chances that she and Maggie would be chosen in the lottery. What Jade didn't know was that we were already running certain algorithms to ensure that only the most likely candidates were under serious consideration. The pool she was trying to increase was actually smaller than she knew. Which is why I'm happy to announce that I did a little digging and determined that both Jade and Maggie won their places fairly. Their original entry was selected in both cases."

"That seems unlikely," Braxon muttered.

"Are you doubting my word, beloved?" Phaedra smiled sweetly at her *mahoyen*.

"Never. If you say it is so, that's how it is," Braxon relented with a hint of a smile.

Everyone else nodded in agreement. Striker didn't believe for one moment that Phaedra was telling the truth, but he was grateful for the lie. It was another way to make sure no one questioned Maggie's citizenship.

"That's the good news. Now, for the bad. Jade wasn't the only one trying to manipulate the outcome. I found another subprogram buried in the software. It was so subtle I almost missed it. Worse, the moment I started poking at it, the damned thing tore itself apart and vanished before I got a decent look at it."

"Self-destructing code?" River asked. "That sounds like…"

"The Gray Men. Yeah. That's what I was thinking, too. I have a few images I was able to capture before it was gone. I've sent them to a friend. If anyone can figure out who created the code, he can."

The room fell silent. The Gray Men were a shadowy organization with a long history of causing problems for the cyborgs. They'd been responsible for creating them in the first place, and Reamus Station had been one of their research bases.

"Why would they care about a list of human colonists? None of the corporations gave a damn about us before. Why now?" Maggie asked.

"I can think of a few reasons. The most obvious one being they want to know what's going on here." Phaedra looked around the room, her normally sunny face grim. "I think we have to assume they were trying to plant a spy."

"Who?" Edge demanded. The question was echoed all around the room by the others.

"I don't know. The code destroyed itself before I could figure that out. I don't even know if they were successful."

"We have to assume they were," Tyran said, his voice carrying all the weight of his royal training.

"Which means we have seven human colonists we need to keep an eye on," Phaedra agreed.

"You mean eight," River said.

"Seven. One of the colonists has officially requested to be taken back to Earth. On paper, Kara Farrow appeared to be everything we were looking for, but it's come to our attention that now we need to change our selection criteria to ensure future applicants demonstrate a strong ability to adapt to new circumstances." Phaedra winked at Maggie. "This life isn't for everyone."

"So that's it? We think we might have a spy, but we can't be sure?"

"For now, yes. We can't send everyone else back just because one of them might be an agent for the Grays. We knew this was a risk when we started discussing this plan. Nothing has changed," Denz said.

"One thing has. Whatever happens, we'll be keeping a closer eye on all our applicants from Earth. If they tried once, they'll try again. It might be Torex Mining, too. Or some other faction we haven't considered. According to the one surviving member of the mercenaries who attacked Maggie, they did a lot of work for various corporations, including Torex. Nothing on the ship's computers could confirm that, though."

"And the ship?" River asked.

"Is now the property of the colony. Legal savage. All the paperwork has been signed as of an hour ago," Denz said.

"And the prisoner?" Maggie asked. "I know he was part of the crew, but I never laid eyes on him, and Jade said he tried to sneak her extra food when he could. I don't think he's a bad person."

"Cameron Allen wasn't a member of the mercenary team. He ran the galley and cleaned up after the other crew for the most part, and it wasn't a voluntary position. The kid was included as chattel for a debt some Jeskyran owed the merc captain. We checked his story and confirmed the details. He was an indentured servant on a twenty-year contract," Denz explained.

"How? I thought slavery was illegal?" River asked.

"Slavery is. Indentured service isn't. That gray area allows unscrupulous assholes to take control of beings' lives and claim it's legal." Denz scrubbed a hand through his dark hair. "If the council is in agreement, I'd like to suggest we offer Cameron Allen a place here in Haven and give him a chance to earn his citizenship, just like the other colonists."

A buzz ensued around the room, and not all of it was positive.

"Not today. He's still being debriefed and will remain under house arrest until we're sure he's not a threat. I mean eventually. It's not like we have a jail here, anyway. Where would we hold him? And on what grounds? We've only got a basic legal system in place right now. If you want to start trying people for crimes, we're going to need to write up a criminal code first."

"Let's table that for today," Edge said. "I for one do not want to spend the next three hours talking about a legal system."

"Agreed," Tyran said amid a murmur of relief.

"Back to the spy issue for a moment," Phaedra said. "For now, I think we should agree not to discuss it with anyone outside this room. If the others knew, they'd never accept the new arrivals and everything we're working toward would fall apart. None of us want that." With that, Phaedra sat down, leaving everyone to talk quietly for a few minutes.

When Tyran called for a vote, every council member voted to keep it a secret for the time being. No one seemed happy at the idea of keeping secrets, but for now, it was the best thing they could do.

"And that brings us to our last bit of business," Edge announced. "I've been asked to bring forward a request to form a new kind of organization. Their purpose would be multifold. Mapping the land around the colony and documenting the flora and fauna of this world would be two of these goals. The other would be the protection of the colony and its citizens from any threat that might manifest from either this world or forces outside it."

"Are you talking about a military?" Tyran asked.

Striker got to his feet. "Not really. We don't need a military presence, but what happened with Maggie and the mercenaries made it clear we need some kind of rapid response team to deal with threats. The *kopaki* and ghost cats are going to kill someone someday if no one deals with them," he explained.

"And I bet none of you even know what a bark spider is, but they're venomous and could kill anyone without nanotech enhancement," Maggie chimed in.

Everyone turned to stare at her. "What the *fraxx* is a bark spider, and why is this the first I'm hearing about them?" Denz asked, looking slightly horrified.

In answer, Striker linked to the hologram projector and sent several pictures of the creatures to the display, including one that showed his arm after being bitten.

"I'm sorry I asked," Denz muttered.

"That's in the forest? Here?" Phaedra shook her head. "Nope. That's it. We're going to need to burn down the whole thing and start over again."

Raze leaned forward with interest. "Never seen one of those on my side of the mountains. Nasty."

"I think Striker and Maggie just made the need for a ranger program very apparent," Edge said. "Striker, will you be organizing this?"

"I will. It will be open to any colonist who is interested in learning how to protect us from any threats while protecting the environment from our presence here."

"If any of you could see what my species did to our home planet, you'd understand how important this will be for the future of the colony." Maggie stood up and took his hand. It was something they'd both agreed was important to them. For now, they'd both keep their jobs in town, but this was something they were committed to doing to help the colony thrive.

The first day he'd seen Maggie, he'd been sure of two things. She and every other human on that shuttle were a threat to the planet and the colony, and she was an outsider, just like him.

He couldn't have imagined the day would come when they'd stand together, hand in hand, and take on the task of protecting the woods of Haven together... and that neither of them would be outsiders anymore.

Ignoring everyone around them, he gathered her into his arms and kissed her, enjoying the flash of surprise in her eyes. She hummed softly against his lips and wrapped her fingers in his shirt, holding him in place as she kissed him back.

Denz laughed. "Since there appears to be no further information coming from Striker, I think we can move on to the vote. All in favor of the creating of the ranger program, raise your hands."

By the time he broke their kiss, the votes were cast.

"Congratulations. You've got yourself a program. Any idea who you're recruiting for it?" Edge asked.

"Wreckage, Ruin, and Axe for a start. I want to talk to some Vardarians, too.

"And me," Maggie said firmly.

"And Maggie. And then we'll see who wants to be part of this. It'll be open to anyone willing to put in the work."

"Even humans?"

Maggie growled a little. Striker thought it was adorable. "Even humans," he confirmed.

"One day, you're going to have to learn to stop being such a judgmental ass," River said as she moved past Edge on her way to the door. "I hope I'm there to see it when someone finally teaches you that lesson."

"And someday, you're going to take that stick out of your…" Edge trailed off when he saw Phaedra and Denz both glaring at him. "Right. Sorry. No insulting fellow council members, even if they started it."

"I swear. I'm bringing a stun baton to the next meeting. First one to get out of line *zap!*" Phaedra muttered.

"You will do no such thing, little warrior. You are not even on the council," Tyran reminded her.

"See? That's an even better reason to let me. I'm not going to interfere with council politics that way. I'm just an unbiased enforcer." She eyed the seats around the table. "I could wire the chairs to emit a low voltage shock instead…"

"That female scares me," Edge murmured and then headed for the exit.

"He's smarter than he looks," Maggie observed once Edge was out of earshot.

"Sometimes." He glanced down at his mate. "Ready to celebrate?"

"Yes!" She raised her voice. "Drinks at the Bar None for everyone. First round is on me."

Cheers, laughter, and promises to see them at the tavern followed them out into the night air. They walked in silence, hand in hand.

They were on the bridge with the Bar None in sight when Maggie came to a sudden stop.

"What is it?" he asked when he saw her standing still, staring up at the sky.

"I… is that snow?" she asked as a gust of wind sent a fresh flurry of snowflakes dancing around them.

He had barely noticed the weather until she pointed it out. "It is. Why?"

"I've… never seen it before. It's beautiful."

As far as he was concerned, there wasn't anything in the universe more lovely than the woman standing with wide eyes, staring up into the night sky, hands outstretched to catch the flakes as they fell.

"Tomorrow, we'll go for a walk in it. You, me, and a few hours in the woods. Sound good?"

She beamed at him. "Sounds perfect."

He wrapped an arm around her shoulders and set off toward the tavern. Perfection wasn't something he'd ever expected to find in his life… but somehow he had, and she was walking beside him.

"Did you invite everyone to the party already?"

"I have. Wreckage wanted to know if Jade would be there. I told him she wasn't even out of the healer's care yet. But maybe next time. He and Ruin will see us there."

"Great. I want to thank everyone who helped you get to us in time."

"So do I." Without them, he might have lost the best thing to come into his life.

Ahead of them, someone opened the door to the tavern, filling the air with noise and light. He caught hold of her hand and led her toward it. He had a lot to be grateful for tonight. It was time to start celebrating.

Thank You for Reading Her Cyborg Champion!

Keep reading for a bonus scene from book three - Her Alien Forgemasters

I hope you enjoyed Striker and Maggie's story.
If you're looking for more stories like this one, I invite you
to explore the other books in the <u>Drift</u> universe, which
now Include Haven Colony, <u>Nova Force</u> and the original
<u>Drift</u> series.

BONUS SCENE - ANYA

Anya had enjoyed a string of good days since coming to Haven, but this one was even better than usual. Her bar was packed, the patrons were all behaving, and everything was working the way it should.

The moment she had that thought, she rapped her knuckles three times on the top of the bar to ward off any bad luck that might be tempted by her open invitation to cause havoc. She'd had more than her share of chaos before coming here, and she had no doubt there'd be more in her future. Just… not right now. Tonight they all wanted to celebrate.

Every citizen of Haven knew the story of how this place had come to be, and how many factions would like to see them fail. Torex Mining Corp wanted their planet back so they could tear it apart to reach the rich veins of tantalum buried beneath the surface. Darker forces wanted to reclaim their lost "property," the cyborgs they had imprisoned and experimented on in their mad quest to build a better soldier.

And then there were the Vardarians. Thousands of

them had followed Prince Tyran to Haven to start a new life far from the boundaries of their empire. She didn't have to know the details to know there was a reason so many beings uprooted their lives to travel across the stars and start their lives over again.

One thing she'd learned in her life was that beings were the same the galaxy over. It didn't matter what sect, class, or species they were, intelligent life all seemed to follow the same patterns. Most of them tried to be good, even if they often failed, and some of them always reached for more than they should have. Power, wealth, influence. When it reached a certain point, the decent ones always left and tried to start over somewhere new… and then the whole dance started over again.

That's what Haven was—the first steps in a dance that might end in a year, a decade, or a few millennia. There was no way to know, and that was part of the magic. All she could be certain of was that here and now was her best chance to be a part of something special. It's what Phaedra had offered her, along with the unvarnished truth about the challenges Anya would face if she came. Unstable cyborgs who distrusted humans, a new species no one knew much about, and a new world that hadn't even been surveyed properly.

She'd said yes in a heartbeat.

Now she had a booming business and a sense of community she'd never known before. These beings weren't just her customers. They were her friends and neighbors. And tonight, they'd gathered to celebrate the newest addition to their ranks. After being claimed by Striker, Maggie was now officially a citizen of Haven, the first of the human refugees to reach that status. As far as Anya was concerned, no one deserved happiness more than Maggie. It made her heart happy to hear her friend's laughter and watch her lean into Striker's side, her joy an almost tangible thing that lifted everyone around her.

"She glows," Saral said as she placed a plate of snacks in front of Anya. "It's nice to see."

"It is."

"So would seeing you eat. You work too hard and don't take care of yourself. You need to find a good male or two to make sure you are well cared for."

"That is your answer to everything. Males are not the cure to all the troubles of the universe."

"No. True. They are also the cause of many of them. But the orgasms help." Saral laughed and touched her hand. "You'll see when you meet your destiny."

"Bah. My destiny is to grow old and rich running this place. Which won't happen if my best cook is out of the kitchen much longer. Shoo!"

The Vardarian female retreated to her domain again, still laughing softly. As happy as Saral was with her mates, she couldn't see that not everyone was destined for that kind of love. Some, like Anya, just didn't seem easy to love, and that was fine by her. She knew her flaws and accepted them because they were part of who she was. She'd been around long enough to learn to like the woman she'd become.

"And I don't have time for a man, anyway. I barely have time for me."

The droids had the orders covered, so she took her plate and retreated to the end of the bar to eat. Not long after, the door opened and two new faces walked into her bar. She'd never seen either of them before.

Single she might be, but she wasn't blind. If she'd laid eyes on either of these males before, she'd remember. They were both Vardarian, one silver-skinned, the other golden. The silver one was a hand span taller than his companion, but even the shorter of them had to be well over two meters tall.

When they removed their coats, she got an eyeful of powerful shoulders and arms that dwarfed even the other Vardarians present. No arm band either, which meant they were unmated. The taller one was blond with a broad smile and rugged features while the golden one kept his expression guarded and moved with care between the tables, avoiding even the slightest contact with the other patrons.

She knew the look. He was used to having to work to avoid trouble or notice, though with his size, she couldn't imagine who or what would dare to take issue with him.

They were almost to the back of the room where Maggie and Striker were holding court when the dark-haired one stopped and turned around. He took a deep breath, his massive chest rising as he sucked in a lungful of air.

Fraxx. She knew what that meant. The male had caught a scent that intrigued him. It might be the roasted *gharshtu* on special tonight, or it could mean he'd detected the scent of his mate.

When he started looking around the room, she knew dinner wasn't what had his interest.

"Here we go again." She watched, curious to see who it would be. Several Vardarian females were present tonight, along with a large group of cyborg women who were celebrating with Maggie. Who was about to have their lives turned upside down?

When the big male's gaze landed on her, she expected him to take one look and keep moving.

He didn't. His amber eyes brightened, and he took another breath.

Oh, hell no.

A second later, the blond spun around to stare at her, too.

Anya took a step back. This was not happening. She'd known when she agreed to come here that as a single female this was theoretically possible, but she'd never for one second thought she'd be some Vardarians' mate.

Both males stalked toward her, their skin gleaming like newly minted coins as their scales tightened, a sure sign they were agitated.

So was she.

"*Mahaya,*" the blond one said, his voice a deep rumble.

"Ma-hay-nope," she retorted. "I serve the food, but I am not on the menu."

"But you are our *mahaya,*" the dark-haired one spoke this time, and his voice was pitched like rolling thunder.

Damn. He was sexy. They both were. If they'd been looking for a night of no-strings-attached sex, she might have been tempted. But this?

It had to be a mistake.

Both males stepped forward at the exact same moment. As they reached out to her, she noted they bore a matching pair of circular scars on their wrists. They were *anrik*, a blood-bonded pair.

"I can't be. There has to be a mistake."

"No mistake," the blond said. "I am Tra'var. This is my *anrik*, Damos. What is your name?"

"Anya. Anya Hutchinson."

"Anya." Damos spoke the word with all the intensity of a prayer. "Shining star. It suits you."

"It does?"

"Oh yes." Tra'var reached for her again.

"Come. We have a lot to discuss and not much time."

To her surprise, Anya stepped forward and took their hands as if it was the most natural thing in the world to do, despite the fact that every sensible cell in her brain was screaming at her to run for the hills before it was too late.

"Finally!" Saral exclaimed from the kitchen door, her smile as bright as a binary star system. "Go with them, Anya. We'll take care of this place. You… enjoy yourself. Oh, your mother will be so pleased!"

"Do not tell my mother anything!" The last thing she needed was Hezza to cut short her cargo run so she could stick her nose into Anya's business. If this was happening, the last thing in the galaxy she needed was her mother's help.

She could screw this up all on her own…

Want to know what happens next?
Her Alien Forgemasters is out this fall

ABOUT THE AUTHOR

Susan lives out on the Canadian west coast surrounded by open water, dear family, and good friends. She's jumped out of perfectly good airplanes on purpose and accidentally swum with sharks on the Great Barrier Reef.

If the world ends, she plans to survive as the spunky, comedic sidekick to the heroes of the new world, because she's too damned short and out of shape to make it on her own for long.

You can find out more about Susan and her books at:
www.susanhayes.ca